MY DAD WROTE A

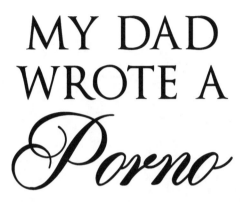

WROTE A

Porno

THE FULLY ANNOTATED EDITION OF

Belinda Blinked 1;

JAMIE MORTON, JAMES COOPER,
ALICE LEVINE, AND
ROCKY FLINTSTONE

G

Gallery Books

New York   London   Toronto   Sydney   New Delhi

G

Gallery Books
An Imprint of Simon & Schuster, Inc.
1230 Avenue of the Americas
New York, NY 10020

Copyright © 2016 by Jamie Morton, James Cooper, Alice Levine, and Rocky Flintstone
Belinda Blinked 1 copyright © 2015 by Rocky Flintstone and is used here with permission
First published in Great Britain in 2016 by Quercus Editions Limited
Published by arrangement with Quercus Editions Limited

First Gallery Books hardcover edition September 2017

GALLERY BOOKS and colophon are registered trademarks of Simon & Schuster, Inc.

For information about special discounts for bulk purchases, please contact Simon & Schuster Special Sales at 1-866-506-1949 or business@simonandschuster.com.

The Simon & Schuster Speakers Bureau can bring authors to your live event. For more information or to book an event, contact the Simon & Schuster Speakers Bureau at 1-866-248-3049 or visit our website at www.simonspeakers.com.

Manufactured in the United States of America

10 9 8 7 6

Library of Congress Cataloging-in-Publication Data is available.

ISBN 978-1-5011-8069-9
ISBN 978-1-5011-8070-5 (ebook)

Thanks to the Belinkers for making this happen.
Thanks to Mum for letting this happen.

Foreword

Fathers and sons. It's a complicated relationship. Oedipus and Laius. Darth Vader and Luke Skywalker. Jesus and God.

But those guys don't have shit on me.

When my own sixty-year-old father, with a devilish sparkle in his eye, informed me he'd written his first novel, little did I know my life would change forever. In my naivety I was encouraging, supportive, even proud.

What an idiot.

From the moment my eyes scanned the first sentence it became instantly clear this was no swashbuckling tale of pirates on the high seas, no espionage spy series with gadgets and cars.

This was porn.

Well, erotica, to be fair to him. But the sexual fantasies of the man who took you fishing and shares a bed with your mother aren't something you want to engage in. Ever. I slammed the laptop shut, unsure if I could ever unsee the first chapter.

My childhood died that day. Death by dad-porn. My world was in freefall and it wasn't long before the five stages of grief visited me in turn:

DENIAL

It couldn't be true. *Belinda Blinked 1* had to be a joke. The man's a retired builder from Northern Ireland, for God's sake. He has as much knowledge of porn as Mary Berry. Just because he's heard of *Fifty Colors of Grey* (as he calls it) doesn't mean he's the heir to E. L. James. I've been to Wimbledon; it doesn't make me Rafael Nadal.

ANGER

How could he do this to me? To my sisters. To my mum. Granted, he'd adopted a creative pen name. But how far could Rocky Flintstone really protect us from the ridicule of the world? A pseudonym does little to numb the pain of having a porn baron for a father, believe me.

BARGAINING

It's not too late—I can reason with him. As fun as this undoubtedly was, he must realize the damage his randy ramblings could do—divorce rates are soaring as it is. But perhaps a more pressing concern is, why the pots-and-pans industry?! Is that really the best setting for a steamy tale of sex and "dripping passion"? Vom.

DEPRESSION

He's self-published it on Amazon. Great. It's real now. And anyone can find it courtesy of the three Google tags he's employed: erotica, lesbian, and business and leadership. So it's both a carnal caper and business studies manual?! Hysterical in one breath, tragic in the other. I just can't shake the deep-rooted despair churning my stomach daily. Why? Just why?

ACCEPTANCE

OK, so he's written a porno. So what? Man up, Jamie—you should read the bloody thing before you judge it. It might be good? It might be . . . sexy.

But I can't read it alone. No, that would be just too weird. There's safety in numbers, and so in a vague attempt at retaining my sanity, I roped in my mates James and Alice to share the burden with me. We braced ourselves, we bulk-bought beer, and together we tentatively dipped our toes into the devilish mind of my ever so slightly perverted father.

And what a mind.

From the word go, as you're about to discover, we knew we had stumbled upon a gold mine of literary shambolics. This was no Jilly Cooper. This was better. The grammar, the lexicon, the boldness with which Flintstone pushes the boundaries of conventional syntax is revolutionary.

And the sex. This is imagery the likes of which you've never heard. And for good reason. Honestly, if I didn't exist I'd question whether my dad had ever even had sex.

And what of our protagonist? The titular character herself, Belinda Blumenthal. She's a results-driven businesswoman with a penchant for unorthodox tactics with which to secure her "deals." She'll literally do anything to sign a client. Imagine a woman with the determination of Hillary Clinton, the business acumen of Karen Brady, and the sexual appetite of Jenna Jameson.

That's our Belinda. One of the greatest heroines in English literature.

I bet you can hardly contain your excitement. And a good thing too, because we've reached the moment. It's time. Strap yourself in, charge your glasses, and prepare to enter the world of *Belinda Blinked 1*, my dad's smutty work of genius. Enjoy.*

Jamie

*If that's in any way possible.

Belinda Blinked 1;

My dad doesn't even own a mobile phone.

Oh good Lord, are there more?

A MODERN STORY OF SEX, EROTICA AND PASSION;

How the sexiest sales girl in business earned her huge bonus by being the best at removing her high heels.

This is JUST the title? Could barely fit that on Twitter.

Is he sponsored by semicolons?

AUTHOR:

ROCKY FLINTSTONE:

And now a colon. Natch.

Chapters;

Brassiere (n) Early twentieth century: From French *brassiere*, literally "bodice or child's vest."

Basically he wants
her in a posh bra.

This is classic Dad—he's obsessed
with inanimate objects when he's
trying to turn people on.
Who cares about the coatracks?

CHAPTER 1

The Job Interview;

Drink! (See page 207 for the official drinking-game rules.)

Belinda blinked, it wasn't a dream, the job interviewer had just asked her to remove her jacket and silk blouse. The Managing Director across the desk who had innocently brought her through from reception smiled and nodded at her. Slowly with the hint of a tease, Belinda removed the two garments. Her black brassiere was doing overtime to contain her full breasts, she had worn this one for today as it was tight fitting on purpose... she never thought it would be exposed in such a simple way.

Even her tits are business-minded.

The MD got up and took her blouse and jacket. He hung them onto one of two elegant wooden coat racks in the corner and sat back down. What next Belinda thought?

The interviewer resumed his questioning of her CV and after about five minutes, asked her to remove her knee length skirt. Belinda stood up, removed the offending garment and passed it with some surprise to the MD.

Surprise? Why? She's removed everything else!

Can I please take this opportunity to apologize. To everyone.

Because her socks have gone.

So, she's as surprised at getting the job as she is when she's asked to remove her skirt?

Dad, little tip—no woman wants their breasts to nosedive to their knees.

Clearly—anyone who gets naked in a job interview is pure class.

Underneath she was wearing a skimpy black thong and sexy black stockings which she didn't apologize for, after all she was an upmarket woman. She sat down again and crossed her long legs. She knew they looked good, but she really felt she wanted to keep her private pussy area hidden. Belinda leaned back on the white leather seat and started to gently sweat.

Erotic. There's nothing sexier than a sweaty lady.

After a further ten minutes of questioning the MD got up and walked round to Belinda, he gently pulled her stockings down to her ankles. He removed her bright red high heels and stuffed the stockings inside them. They were placed under the coat rack by the interviewer. Belinda was now feeling exposed, with only a bra and thong left, she thought total nakedness was not far away, and then what?

Her skin?!

The MD then surprised her by saying they wanted to offer her the job as their Sales Director today on completion of a few further details. Belinda was surprised as the job was worth £85,000 a year plus car and all the travel perks, so she nodded her head. With her agreement given the MD walked behind her and unhooked the tight black bra in a rapid movement, Belinda's breasts plunged to freedom and her nipples immediately stood to attention.

Wait, she agreed to the job, not stripping.

The MD sat down and appraised her, whilst the interviewer calmly asked her to stand up and remove her thong. Her shaven pussy was revealed with just a delicate runway of dark pubic hair guiding any viewer to the top of her vagina.

If you need guiding there you've already gone wrong.

I've never thought of a vagina as a Tupperware box.

Language Alert

Runnel (n) late sixteenth century (denoting a brook or rill), variant of dialect "rindle," influenced by the verb "run." _Or could just be a typo . . ._

How is HR in the room? Starting the petition to get Bill fired immediately.

Talking Point

Notice that this is the first time in the novel that Belinda speaks. What does Flintstone's choice of dialogue say about her character?

How is Bill not fired yet?

Drink!

Oh. Holy. Jesus.

'Now sit down and relax Miss Blumenthal.' said the interviewer. 'In fact, just spread your legs wide so we can get a good look at your internal attributes.'

Belinda lay back in the leather chair and spread her legs wide as requested. Her vaginal lids popped open and her labial pinkness was there for them to assess. She quickly became moist and a runnel of liquid trickled down her left lower thigh.

What a great time for introductions! She's starkers and now he reveals his name.

The MD then said, 'My name is Tony, and you will report directly to me. Bill here is our Human Resources Director and he's available to you at all times. You might need him as you have a direct staff of 28, some of whom may need fucking off!'

Belinda nodded and asked, which, was to her the obvious question, 'When are you guys going to fuck me?' Tony quickly replied, 'Well, Bill here never will as it's not in his area of responsibility and I might, depending on how hard you work for me. But let's get to the point Belinda, the reason we've put you through this scenario is to ensure your positive reaction to certain members of our customer base who will definitely try you out. So I have to ask you here and now, does this give you any problems?'

Belinda blinked, shook her head and said, 'As long as I have your and the companies backing I will do whatever is necessary to make the sales happen.'

Why do I have a feeling this won't just be her working weekends and taking some paperwork home?

Cultural Context

Etiquette between colleagues varies vastly from culture to culture. The French favor *faire la bise*, or exchanging kisses on both cheeks. The Japanese exercise *eshaku*, a fifteen-degree "greeting" bow.

Giselle and Belinda have forgone convention and opted for the exchanging of fluids. Do you think this a portent for future relations?

I see Dad's misspent youth in the Scouts is rearing its head—be prepared.

Language Alert

Here is another example of the Flintstonean vernacular. His penchant for the word "deft" only draws into sharper focus his ungainly approach to writing.

'Well done Belinda.' said Tony as a large smile crossed his rugged features.

— Yay, Bill's finally fucked off.

Tony then dismissed Bill and said to him as he left the room,

— Literally NO ONE in pots and pans is called Giselle.

'Send in Giselle with the contract.'

Most awkward small talk ever—a few minutes?!

After a few minutes a 26 year old, stunningly attractive, blonde haired girl joined them with notebook and sheaf of papers in hand.

'Put the paperwork down Giselle and meet Belinda our new Sales Director.'

Giselle's not been brought up right.

Belinda stood up, still totally naked and shook Giselle's hand. In response Giselle held Belinda's face in her hand and kissed her fully square on her lips, Belinda instinctively opened her mouth and Giselle's tongue snaked in and they both shared the touching of ecstasy.

In no way sexy. All I see is Voldemort.

At that magical moment Giselle started to strip off. It didn't take long as she wasn't wearing any underwear and Belinda thought, this girl does this too often for it to be a once in a lifetime event. However Giselle was a magnificent creature, tits that were to die for and an ass that was so tight, even Belinda felt tested, though she was equal in every respect and in all truth felt she had better shaped boobs. With soft deft actions, she soon had Belinda gasping. Belinda could only respond by sucking Giselle's breasts and teething her nipples vigorously. Not a bad final interview for the job of her dreams.

Just enjoy the kiss. Why compare and contrast?

Stop body-shaming, Belinda.

CHARACTER PROFILE: Belinda Blumenthal

Belinda is the female lead: an open-minded woman who is quietly ambitious and meets her targets but uses unorthodox methods to get there. Her career is her main drive.

The world of Steele's Pots and Pans is delivered to us through her blinking eyes.

We meet the eponymous heroine at the apex of her hunt for a new job.

The reader is led to question her reason for seeking new employment.

Belinda's first appearance establishes her as passive, as well as snappily dressed. Though she seems demure and innocent in the initial paragraphs she is soon to be found revealing her "vaginal lids."

Though these submissive themes recur there are active verbs associated with Belinda, such as "blinking," "nodding," and "removing [clothing]." Dialogue is minimal for Blumenthal, her first line not appearing for nine paragraphs ("When are you guys going to fuck me?").

Belinda is refreshingly body confident; she "doesn't apologize" for her sensuality and regards her figure as superior in many ways. Many people have hailed her as the ultimate modern woman.

She is clearly highly qualified as she has made it to the final round of interviews in a competitive market, and then manages to secure the "job of her dreams."

• **Physical Attribute:** Superior breasts to almost everyone

• **Dominant Character Trait:** Passivity and drive in equal measure

• **Unusual Skill:** Her sexual arsenal—which always seals the deal

• **Fun Fact:** She has no friends

🔓 KEY THEME: Pots and Pans

Through the fictional creation of Steele's, Flintstone has lifted the lid on an otherwise unexplored corporate world. As the first novel set in the pots-and-pans industry, *Belinda Blinked 1* grants us unprecedented access into the dark underbelly of kitchenware. Natural comparisons have been drawn between Jordan Belfort (*The Wolf of Wall Street*) and John Niven (*Kill Your Friends*) for their similar revelatory accounts of the trading and music industries.

🎼 KEY MOTIF: Blinking

Winking is traditionally the more provocative and sensual of the eye-closing actions. However, Rocky only realized this once *Belinda Blinked 1* was completed and he could not spare the time to amend every mention (he has since learned of the ctrl + f command). Thankfully he also quite liked the alliteration.

It is not the first time blinking has been misappropriated in literature. There is a theory that the first recorded appearance of the phrase "in the blink of an eye," in the King James Bible, was originally intended to read "in the twinkling of an eye."

Blinking was also attractive to Flintstone as it can be interpreted in many ways. It can be a coquettish advance, a shocked wince, or a confident acknowledgement of a done deal. Blinking also ensures a refreshed water supply to the eyes, protecting them from irritants.

Rocky uses Belinda's blinks to punctuate happenings as a very successful literary device. Her eyes almost take on their own persona, although their color is never revealed.

AUTHOR'S NOTE

Why did you choose the pots-and-pans industry as the business setting for your debut novel?

I've always respected the pots-and-pans trade. In my youth they went from house to house selling their wares . . . effectively tinkers. Door-to-door selling is a hard job and I respect that. In essence I wanted to pay homage to the pots-and-pans sector for the important but very much overlooked contribution they make to our society. If I'm completely honest, I am drawing on all my business experience; the series of novels are all based on events I happened across in my steamy sales world. Of course this is over a period of forty years; don't get the impression this sort of thing was happening to me every day . . . perhaps every other day.

As for Belinda, physically she's based on my hero Angie Harmon, who plays Jane Rizzoli in the smash-hit USA TV series *Rizzoli & Isles*. Belinda herself is truly fictional, but when I was a Ready Mixed Concrete manager many years ago, we had some very attractive ladies call at the depot selling cleaning materials; they would show a bit of leg . . . and get the order. That was awhile ago, of course, and I'm sure this practice doesn't happen today.

Stephen King, my writing inspiration, has always maintained, "write what you know about . . . and make the rest up." Business, and especially the sales environment, was my best bet. That's why everything revolves around the world of business.

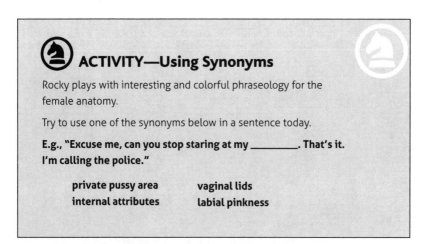

ACTIVITY—Using Synonyms

Rocky plays with interesting and colorful phraseology for the female anatomy.

Try to use one of the synonyms below in a sentence today.

E.g., "Excuse me, can you stop staring at my _____. That's it. I'm calling the police."

private pussy area	**vaginal lids**
internal attributes	**labial pinkness**

Reading group discussion points

- Is Belinda a feminist?

- Discuss the strengths and weaknesses of Belinda's interview technique.

- How does Flintstone use the minutiae, e.g., "elegant wooden coat racks," to distract the reader from the less palatable aspects of the novel?

- Find five examples of breaches of HR protocol.

- Despite his only brief appearance in the chapter, most readers loathe Bill; discuss your thoughts.

- Which character holds the power in this scene?

- Giselle appears before the close of the chapter. What have we learned about her?

Not outraged? Not running to Bill in HR? Not that he'd care. God, I hate Bill.

CHAPTER 2

The Leather Room;

Thank goodness for the clarification that Friday is the day after Thursday.

Three weeks later Belinda had settled into most of the administration parts of the job, but was still to get to grips with the large customer base and her new sales force. It was a typical wet dismal Thursday afternoon at the office and tomorrow, Friday was her first Regional sales meeting where she would discuss sales with her four regional managers. The town hall clock had just chimed three when Giselle called her to Tony's office.

What weird French village is their office in?

'Afternoon Belinda.' said Tony, 'There's a very senior company event on Sunday at our chairman's country house, BBQ and all that. Wear tennis gear… very casual, no and I repeat no undergarments such as thongs or bra.

If she's actually going to play tennis I fear for her eyes.

Belinda looked up now intrigued. Tony smiled and said… 'You'll understand when you get there! I'll get Giselle to book you a room for Sunday night at the local hotel. It's called the Horse and Jockey. OK? It's probably best if you check in before you get to the old man's place.'

With a secret door I see Dad's love of
James Bond is shining through... ———————

Belinda's always thinking
of the bottom line. ———————

It's the classic tale:
Boy interviews girl.
Boy strips girl.
Girl gets job.
Boy ignores girl. ———————

Talking Point

Professionalism is a running virtue in *Belinda Blinked 1*.
Note how often Flintstone uses proficiency in business as
a representation of a character's worth.

Belinda nodded, 'I can certainly rearrange my shopping trip to Saturday. Oh and I'll not bother purchasing any thongs or bras!' She smiled sweetly and Tony laughed.

Doesn't she own any already?

'Good, go through to my leather room whilst I get Giselle'. Tony opened what looked like a normal cupboard door in the corner of his office and switched on some delicate lighting. Belinda went in and the door shut behind her.

How can lighting be delicate?

'Wow!' she thought, Tony wasn't joking, this was her first visit to this part of the offices and the entire room including the floor was covered in exquisite leather tiles, they must have cost a fortune. There was no other furniture except an extremely sophisticated and expensive drinks cabinet in the corner.

I love that a drinks cabinet is more sophisticated than Belinda.

'What does he get up to in here?' she thought.

Sex, Belinda.

Belinda realized that she might find out sooner than she bargained for. Anyway, what did it matter, she had been surprised that he hadn't come onto her since that final interview. After all he was a good looking single guy and was very professional in his approach to the business. With his astute guidance she had successfully installed herself as Sales Director and was now preparing her strategy on some major accounts, again with his help.

Hang on, Giselle was twenty-six last chapter—
this is like some shit GCSE maths problem.
If Hardeep has twenty-four sweets in a bag
and four of them are orange, and Jenny eats
two of them, how old is Giselle?

Talking Point

Playwright Michael Shurtleff famously said, "Conflict is
what creates drama." Here Flintstone stops any potential
intrigue in its tracks. What does this do to raise or lower
the stakes of the novel?

How are Giselle's nicotine-stained,
grubby talons scratching at Belinda's
breasts sexy?

Belinda thought about Giselle, she was probably Tony's preferred taste in
women, five years younger than herself at 24, Giselle was <u>blonde</u> not dark
like Belinda, She was Tony's PA and right hand man, foreign, of Dutch
nationality, and probably the successor to Tony as MD in four or five years
when Tony moved up in the company hierarchy. Belinda was not interested
in becoming MD so no conflict would ever exist between her and Giselle.
This was probably a good thing for her longevity with the outfit.

Like a budget Marilyn Monroe.

How small is this company? PA to MD in five years? That's quite the meteoric rise.

Belinda's thoughts were interrupted when the door opened and Giselle
walked in.

Really? Plural?

'Hi Belinda, what do you think of his "fucking leather room"?'

Belinda smiled and said, 'I could do with a <u>drink</u>....'

Tell me about it.

Giselle walked over to the drinks cabinet, poured two stiff Gin and Tonics
and started to stroke Belinda's tits with her long fingernails. Belinda felt
herself respond and took a swift drink while she still could. Unasked she put
her tongue into Giselle's mouth.

Unasked? Does Giselle require written permission?

'That tastes good' said Giselle as she removed Belinda's jacket and skirt.
Belinda slipped the straps of Giselle's dress down her arms and in a swift
movement removed the whole dress.

Dad's always been inspired by the 1980s tablecloth trick.

Cultural Context

Occupations where undressing is integral to job efficiency include:

• Theater dressers

• Triathletes

• Prostitutes

Sales directors are not usually required to be adept in the removal of clothing at pace.

Language Alert

Deft (a) Neatly skillful and quick in one's movements.

A Flintstone favorite. Keep a tally of every reference to this word throughout *Belinda Blinked 1*.

Cultural Context

Gwyneth Paltrow's popular lifestyle website Goop suggests women should indulge in a v-steam, where a "combination of infrared and mugwort steam cleanses your uterus, et al. It is an energetic release that balances female hormone levels."

UP?! Where? Is she wearing her bra as shoulder pads?

'Very professional Belinda.' said Giselle as she again turned her attention to Belinda's tits. It only took Giselle a second to remove Belinda's satin blouse and push up her bra cups. Belinda's nipples started to swell in anticipation before Giselle's lips and teeth started to punish them.

Sounds like her nipples have gone into anaphylactic shock.

It took about as much time for Belinda to unhook Giselle's bra and then slip her knickers to the floor. Giselle deftly stepped out of them and kicked her heels to the side of the room.

'Lie down on the floor Belinda, and enjoy all that leather.' said the now completely naked Giselle.

Belinda did as she was told as well as pulling off her bra. Now stretched out on the floor with only her thong in place Belinda was game for anything… besides what else would she be doing on a wet Thursday afternoon, twelve hours before her first Regional Sales meeting?

God forbid her job.

claws

Giselle's ~~hands~~ soon made light work of Belinda's thong. The two girls started to excite each other and soon their respective vaginas were wet and steaming. They took it in turns to lick each other's clits and when Tony entered the room they were both ready for a bit of male interaction.

That phrase has never been written down EVER.

19

There's a joke to be made about discussing Tony's
lunch box while Belinda tucks into her lunch box,
but I'll leave that kind of thing to Dad.

How can a thong be wonky?
Unless you've got a crooked
arse crack, of course.

Language Alert

Typos are another key trait of the Flintstonean lexicon.

However, it can be argued that Flintstone's choice of
spelling is deliberate, with it embodying the dizzy
disorientation Belinda is experiencing in the moment.

Talking Point

Belinda's breasts have been scratched, scraped, and scored. Now red-raw,
an appropriate treatment would be the application of calamine lotion. Often
prescribed for sunburn, insect stings, and poison ivy contact, it would protect
Belinda's chest area from infection. Particularly if she develops weeping or
oozing blisters.

Does that mean he was being enthusiastic or that he'd disappeared up there?!

However Tony had other ideas and just brushed Belinda's body with his hands feeling her responsive breasts and ass. His real objective was Giselle and pretty soon he was deeply into licking her pussy. Meanwhile Giselle was doing the same to Belinda so all in all everyone was getting satisfaction. After about fifteen minutes of this intense activity Belinda excused herself, gathered together her discarded clothes and let herself out of the leather room. Giselle and Tony stayed on for an extra session which Giselle would no doubt enlighten Belinda about at Friday lunch.

It's not a family meal. "Please can I leave the table, Mum?"

Does anyone do ANY work?

Whilst starting to dress in Tony's office the main receptionist Bella walked in and caught Belinda naked adjusting her thong. 'Here, let me do that for you,' said Bella, 'I know how important it is to achieve a straight line with a thong'… look at mine.' Bella hitched up her dress and revealed an even more skimpy thong than Belinda was wearing. Belinda stroked Bella's ass in appreciation and thought the obvious… not another one! What is this office running on… high powered sexual adrenelin?

A handshake would suffice.

Bella turned round and caressed Belinda's substantial tits which were still suffering from Giselle's attentions. Belinda responded by putting her hand between Bella's legs, pushing Bella's thong to one side so she could finger her clit. Bella groaned and started kissing Belinda's mouth.

I can't believe my dad has written "finger her clit."

'Help me dress' gasped Belinda, not wanting to be discovered by Tony and Giselle exiting the leather room, which Bella had probably no idea existed.

That's the second time she's pissed on the parade today.

How dumb is Bella if she doesn't?

Lest we forget, they
don't even know each
other's names. ——————————

It's just been available twice. And she didn't
"take it in good stead" either time. ——————

I love that going home is her
favorite part of the job. ——————

Bella took the hint and calmed down, taking inordinate pleasure in placing Belinda's bra and stockings onto her smooth body.

'Let's do this again and in private.' said Belinda. Bella nodded whilst straightening Belinda's thong for the last time and picked up the correspondence she had gone to Tony's office to collect for the last post.

It's not a tie.

Finally a worker bee.

'I'll hold you to that Belinda,' said Bella, 'My place next Friday evening, say 9.00pm.'

'It's a date!' Belinda replied, wondering how she'd have the sexual strength to get through the next week, but instinctively she knew if sex was made available then she'd take it all in good stead.

Belinda went to her office and picked up her briefcase. On the desk was an agenda with client attendance details of the Sunday bash at the Chairman's house. It would make interesting reading that night when she got back to her apartment as well as the final preparations for her Regional Sales Manager meeting in the morning. Outside in the car park Belinda jumped into her two week old Mercedes coupe. Swish and expensive, Belinda so loved this part of the job. She gunned the engine and drove the twenty minutes to her new central London apartment.

Clearly just for show.

Probably more interesting than this chapter.

WHERE THE HELL IS THIS?

⬤ CHARACTER PROFILE: Giselle

Giselle is the PA of Steele's Pots and Pans and Tony's right-hand man in more ways than one. Indeed she is embroiled in an ambiguous affair with her boss, though they are yet to formally label their relationship.

Stunningly attractive with hair as yellow as the sun and an ass so tight it tests even the lithest of colleagues, Giselle is a Dutch beauty. Young at only twenty-six or twenty-four, she is keen to avoid being tied down and is game for anything.

Despite her demure appearance, she harbors a steely determination befitting the namesake of her parent company. Her ambition knows no bounds and her sparkling blue eyes are firmly set on becoming Tony's successor in a mere five years' time. She infuses every action with purpose and drive as razor-sharp as her impossibly long fingernails.

Paradoxically she is never happier than when she is shunning her workload and engaging in illicit sexual liaisons, be it in broad view of the wider office or in a shrouded "fucking leather room." She'll relish any opportunity to show off her very tight posterior and attractive breasts, though they're inferior to Belinda's in shape.

- **Physical Attribute:** Long fingernails

- **Dominant Character Trait:** Ferociously ambitious

- **Unusual Skill:** Getting marks out of leather

- **Fun Fact:** She's sleeping with the boss

KEY THEME:
Interior Design, the Role of Leather

For centuries leather has been entrenched in the erotic milieu. From the whips and bondage collars of BDSM, to the jackets donned by the T-Birds in *Grease*, cowhide has aroused generations.

However, its prominence in interior design is less celebrated. Leather has featured in many buildings, often serving as the bridge between class and smut. The House of Commons, the lower house of the UK Parliament, boasts 427 green leather seats on either side of the chamber, and the Batcave enjoyed a padded leather wardrobe in the 1997 bomb *Batman & Robin*. The leather room in *Belinda Blinked 1* is widely believed to be the first and only depiction of an entirely leather-lined room.

Leather experienced a sexual renaissance in the 1970s when the LGBT community embraced the fabric. The inaugural Easter Fetish Week in Berlin served as Europe's biggest gay fetish event, and today leather culture is most prominent in and associated with gay communities. It is unclear if Flintstone is conversant with this particular subculture.

AUTHOR'S NOTE

Why did you decide to create a leather room in the Steele's office?

I've always loved leather: beautiful to touch, divine to smell. Someday someone's going to make a lovely female thong out of it with BELINDA BLINKED printed on it. Besides, it's great on car steering wheels . . . gives fantastic grip, so golfers adore it. It's also waterproof, which makes it ideal for sexual play, such as dildos.

Rocky x

ACTIVITY

Elect three people to engage in a fictitious threesome.

Designate one as "the dominant force," one as "the scratcher," and one as "the most likely to excuse themselves before reaching climax."

 **Reading group discussion points**

- What are the potential risks of an askew thong?

- Steele's Pots and Pans is based near a town hall clock twenty minutes from central London. Can you pinpoint the location of the office?

- It is suggested that Belinda is a little threatened by Giselle in this chapter. Do you think her anxieties are justified?

- As a group, discuss what scenarios could result from a steaming vagina.

- Is Belinda a lesbian? Debate arguments for and against.

Talking Point—The "Boring" Chapter

It is a common technique among erotic novelists to include pauses in the "action" to build anticipation for the next sensual encounter, and *Belinda Blinked 1* is no exception. Chapter 3 is one of the most inane chapters in both the book and in modern literature more generally. "The Regional Sales Meeting" is colloquially referred to as "the ripper," as many copies can be found with this chapter ripped out. The story could easily exist without it.

Probably?? It either is or it isn't, Dad. You're the author—you tell us . . .

Can ANYONE understand this sentence? Answers on a postcard.

Talking Point

Many well-known businessmen and -women have famous mantras that define them. One of Richard Branson's favorite phrases is "Screw it, let's do it." "Done is better than perfect" is the mantra of Facebook COO Sheryl Sandberg, and Coco Chanel is well known for her motto "Keep your heels, head, and your standards high." Interestingly, all of these could be applied to Belinda's approach to her sex life.

Chapter 3

The Regional Sales Meeting;

Belinda had an early breakfast and was in the office for 07.30am. This was probably a pretty important day for her as it would be the first time she would meet her UK senior sales management, in other words the people who reported to her in business terms. She had no particular views… just lots of third party information about the performance and caliber of these four managers. There were also twenty or so salesmen who reported to them on the ground and she had fairly, or unfairly, pessimistic thoughts about how the whole sales organization was performing.

No surprise there. She's the most passive woman in the pots-and-pans industry.

But in sales you can always be surprised, especially when you talked to people in confidence and got them on board… to accept your way of doing things. Belinda was good at this, and Tony knew it… this was probably one of the many reasons he had hired her. There was no major desire in Tony's business plan to sack all the sales force and bring in new people… develop what we have was his mantra.

And the fact she got butt naked in the job interview might have tipped the balance…

Language Alert—Ellipses

The ellipsis is one of the most misunderstood punctuation marks in the English language. In novels it can demonstrate a pause in dialogue, a pause in narrative, or a character or a narrator trailing off.

In Flintstone's case, it seems most likely that he used ellipses as a personal reminder to fill in gaps in detail at a later date, which he then forgot to do.

Talking Point—Where Are the Steele's Pots and Pans Offices?

There is a lot of confusion surrounding the location of Steele's Pots and Pans offices. They are so close to Heathrow Airport that it's impossible to book a taxi as the fee is too low. However, there is a town hall clock close by. Furthermore, Belinda can drive from the office into central London in twenty minutes. But we mustn't forget the drive from Heathrow to central London takes at least forty minutes. Where do you think Belinda's office is based?

Laughed heartily at "cost centre"?!
Gotta get the laughs where you can find them, I suppose.

Basically if they've got a pulse, they can keep their job.

Belinda had already thrashed out a strategy with Tony in her first three weeks of induction to the company… it was simple, if the salesmen and sales managers show any sign of performance then keep them. If not, bite the bullet and dispose. Belinda was tough but not mercenary and she would use all her talents to make the existing sales team work. She just wondered how far she would have to go to get them onside.— *Very, very far.*

Nine-o-clock came and Bella rang her from reception to say the two northerly Regional managers wanted a lift from Heathrow as they couldn't get a taxi to take them to the offices. Classic, Belinda thought, the company locates near Heathrow and you can't get a taxi between the two places as the taxi fare is too low! Belinda picked up the phone to her Sales administration manager, Jim Thompson… her Mr. Fix It in the sales organization. 'Hi Jim, Belinda here, can you rescue my two Regional Sales Managers from the Airport?'

Can't get a taxi from Heathrow?! You should be fired.

Belinda is the pool car of the pots-and-pans industry.

'Be delighted to Belinda, can I take the pool car?' replied Jim.

'Sure,' Belinda replied, 'Just put the cost centre to both of them!'

Jim laughed heartily and said, 'Will do!'

Anyone else think Dave Wilcox
cries during sex? ——————————

Stop using his full name, Belinda
Blumenthal. ——————————

Translation: Are you ready to get naked ... with
your team ... and your customers ... for me? ——————

A knock on Belinda's door saw her London and Home Counties Regional Sales Manager stick his head around the door. 'Pardon the intrusion Ms. Blumenthal, but I'm Des Martin… you know, your London man.'

Belinda got up, 'Des! Great to meet you, grab a seat, we're just picking two of the guys up from Heathrow, which only leaves our man from the West to appear.'

'Ah, you mean Dave Wilcox from Bristol.' said Des.

'I certainly do.' replied Belinda as she sat down behind her desk. 'Oh by the way, call me Belinda from now on.'

'Will do Belinda.' replied Des confidently as he eyed her shapely legs and ass.

She's sat down. How can he see her ass?

Belinda thought, 'I like you Des Martin, confident, sophisticated, good looking, but why the terrible sales performance?' She sighed and leaned back in her chair pushing forward her breasts. 'So Des are you prepared for today? Are you ready to expose yourself, your team and your client base to the new lady and master?'

'Belinda,' said Des, 'If I'm honest it will be the first time anyone in this company has taken an interest in us salesmen instead of bypassing us with corporate deals done from head office over a bottle of whisky.'

Get the violins out, Des! Ever thought that YOU might be the problem?

This is the most Belinda has ever spoken and it's clunky at best. Is English her first language? I preferred it when she was mute.

LITERALLY. NO ONE. CARES.

We're halfway through the chapter and the meeting still hasn't started.

Talking Point—How to Do Business

It is common knowledge that Flintstone intended this book to be both titillating and educational. He wanted it to be a manual on best practice in business. A key piece of advice he delivers is that impressive rooms for meetings are a must. However, as will become clear later, he goes on to suggest that the best way to negotiate large deals is to have sexual intercourse with potential customers. His methods are yet to be endorsed by the wider business world.

Cultural Context

"God's Own Country" was initially used to describe the Wicklow Mountains in Ireland. It has also been used to refer to places in Surrey, Australia, United States, New Zealand, Kerala (India) . . . It is occasionally used to describe Yorkshire.

Belinda looked shocked, 'Tell me you're joking... is this the real story I'm about to find out about today?"

'Put it this way,' said Des, 'you can't say I didn't warn you!' He also thought what a magnificent pair of tits, how long will it take me to get them into my hands and is my job worth it?

A second knock at her office door saw the Western Regional Sales Manager, Dave Wilcox, pop his head around. 'Hope I'm not late, but the traffic on the M4 was desperate!'

'Come on in Dave, I'm Belinda and very nice to meet you!'

Minutes later Jim Thompson rang and told Belinda the two other Regional Sales Managers would be in the car park in three minutes. 'Thanks Jim, get them up to the conference room ASAP and we'll get started for 10.00am.'

The conference room was upmarket, Tony liked to impress those customers who visited the offices and one of the best ways was decent meeting spaces. Jim quickly introduced Patrick O'Hamlin, the Scottish and Ireland Regional Sales Manager and Ken Dewsbury, Regional Sales manager for Central and North England. Both were like chalk and cheese... Patrick was a fast talking Irishman, originally born in Dublin, whilst Ken was from God's own country, South Yorkshire, and sported an accent to match.

Dad is already running out of clichés.

WHY. AM. I. STILL. READING??? ——————

Not sure why Dad's so obsessed with
leather. I don't want to know. ——————

This sounds
like a rubbish
wet T-shirt ——————
competition.

About as subtle as a
brick through a window. ——————

'My God,' thought Belinda, 'What a varied team, surely we can do something with this lot.'

Belinda called the meeting to a halt at noon. Patrick and Dave had each given their hourly presentation, though Belinda could have asked enough questions to extend their presentations to three hours each. However she knew she needed an overview, and the detail could come later in the field when she spent time with each manager individually. Lunch was a quick pint and sandwich in the local pub... The Bull in the Rushes, and as time was of the essence she felt she could only work a little bit of her female magic.

In the ladies toilets, Belinda removed her jacket, blouse and bra, she ran the cold tap and dabbed the water onto her nipples, making them stand to attention. 'That'll have to do for now she thought as she shoved her bra into her leather handbag. She put her blouse back on leaving three of the five buttons undone. She was now showing her cleavage big time and threw her jacket casually over her shoulder. The silken blouse quickly became transparent due to the water and clung longingly to her stunning breasts.

The blouse seems pretty pointless at this stage.

She walked back into the drinking area and observed the effect she had on her new sales team. Only two of her Managers immediately observed her subtle change of attire, and Belinda soon noticed some astute elbowing going around the team, accompanied with wry smiles from the Northerners. Jim was chuckling to himself as he was office based and had

Totally contradicts himself. I
thought Des had a terrible sales
performance? Classic Dad.

Four hours, two locations,
and no progress later, this
is STILL the meeting!

Bloody freeloaders . . .

This company needs to enforce a confidentiality agreement.

heard the rumours put around by Bella and Giselle. Now he could believe them.

The afternoon sessions were equally as professional and Belinda was particularly impressed by Ken Dewsbury, the man showed wit, style and competence in that order. Des Martin was however a true pro, his London bearing and obvious sales talents indicated to Belinda that he was probably her first avenue to finding out how the individual members of the regional sales team ticked.

By the end of the meeting Belinda's blouse had dried out, but her lack of bra and hardened nipples chaffing continually against her tight blouse were still being noticed. Good she thought, let's see who has the guts to make the first move. In her short closing comments which wound down the business side of things, Belinda suggested they all adjourn to the Pentra Hotel which was beside Heathrow airport. That meant the two managers who were on evening flights to Leeds and Glasgow could get off easily and the rest of them could drive home after the rush hour traffic. *Is anyone still reading this??*

Belinda also decided to throw in a couple of wild cards so she asked Giselle and Bella if they would join her team for a couple of drinks on their way home. Both were as keen as mustard when they found out it was all on Belinda's expenses. Jim Thompson drove the three girls over to the Pentra where they met the Regional Sales Managers in the "Long bar" which

WTF does that phrase mean?

Is it a school uniform? Why
has everyone got a blazer on?
And on a separate note, why
will no one wear a bra?

Talking Point
In groups, try to make the sound of a "quiet gasp of admiration."

It's really not appropriate to wap your baps
out in a hotel bar in the early evening.

overlooked the runway. It was now six o clock and the bar was filling up. Jim found seats at a table tucked away in the far corner of the room.

Belinda started the proceedings by taking off her jacket and <u>downing her G&T in one</u>. Bella followed and Giselle "accidently" spilt some of her drink over her blouse, which meant she had to go to the restroom to dry off. In fact, all that came off was her bra and like Belinda earlier that day, she was ready for action with a translucent white blouse and to die for nipples. Jim was on the ball and by the time Giselle had returned he had two replacement G&T's on the table. Bella by now had gathered the "<u>drift</u>" of <u>the drinks session</u> and decided to do her bit for team building. As she wasn't wearing a bra that day she coyly unbuttoned the top three of her blouse buttons and slowly removed her jacket.

<u>Her cleavage was revealed and a</u> quiet gasp of admiration went around the table. Giselle flicked some tonic water at Bella's nipples and soon achieved the desired result. 'Take it off Bella.' Des Martin whispered…'<u>the tonic will stain your blouse</u>… look at Belinda's and Giselle's already!'

Bella smiled and thought, 'Will I be the first? Surely Belinda can't as these guys report to her. Then in a quick movement Bella <u>unbuttoned</u> the rest of her blouse and let her magnificent breasts hang out for all to see.

At the same time? That's quite a party trick.

Has Dad suddenly turned American?

No nipples are worth a human life.

Oh yeah, the TRANSPARENT tonic will stain her blouse.

Fell loose?! She's meant
to be twenty-nine! ——————

Finally, he's decided ——————
to abbreviate it.

Ken Dewsbury choked over his pint of bitter whilst the other three Regional Managers chanted quietly, 'Who's next! Who's next!' Belinda looked at Giselle who nodded and in a leisurely fashion with a big hint of tease unbuttoned the rest of her blouse. Her tits hung freely like pomegranates and she gently massaged them with her hands. 'Come on Belinda!' whispered Ken, "Don't let the sales team down now!'

Dad clearly thought "melons" was too obvious and went for something a bit more . . . exotic.

Belinda smiled, and replied, 'I'll want a 10% increase in your sales next month Ken!'

'Done!' he replied.

Belinda slowly opened the remaining two buttons of her blouse, her tits fell loose, she took a drink and started to massage her nipples with her fingertips. The RSM's all clapped in admiration. Never had they had a sales meeting culminate like this one, things were looking up, and with three pairs of stunning breasts on show, they could do anything.

What, like browsing an old iPod?

A standing ovation seems a little OTT.

Jim Thompson went to get more drinks and the girls started to finger and discuss the merits of each other's nipples.

'Don't make us more jealous girls.' said Patrick O'Hamlin, 'but I've got a plane to catch!'

Feels like that
ship has sailed.

Think this is one of the worst
sentences of the whole novel. One
of the characters isn't in the
book AND the pun is shit.

Talking Point—Who Is Donna?

Readers have always been confused by the sudden, unexplained introduction of a new character here. It raises numerous questions: Who is Donna? What makes her tick? Where has she come from? Did Rocky just accidentally rename Bella briefly?

What a poetic turn of phrase.

'Me too!' said Ken Dewsbury. They both got up, shook everyone's hands and departed with much looking over their shoulders at the line up of tit available at the table. How they wished they both had the guts to <u>finger those breasts.</u> *Fingering? Like poking a jelly to see if it's set?*

The bar was now getting more crowded and Belinda thought it was sensible to button up their blouses, as they didn't want to get <u>accused of being prostitutes.</u> Des Martin and Dave Wilcox drank up, sadly said their goodbyes and disappeared out of the bar.

'Thanks Donna and Giselle you really helped me make a breast of it!' said Belinda laughing. 'One more drink and Jim will get us back to the office.' Jim went back to the bar ordered the drinks and paid the tab. The girls drank up slowly, reliving the looks on each of the Regional Managers faces when they showed them their breasts.

'That was interesting Belinda,' said Donna, 'Any more events like that for us?'

'Let's wait and see,' replied Belinda, 'Let's wait and see!'

I can hardly contain my excitement.

CHARACTER PROFILE:
The Regional Sales Managers

The Regional Sales Managers (or RSMs, as Flintstone inconsistently refers to them) are Belinda's four-man team, overseeing the work of approximately twenty salesmen. As we meet the RSMs, sales at Steele's Pots and Pans are in dire straits. It's clear that these men have become far too safe and comfortable in their jobs, making them complacent and inefficient. Their inability to perform basic tasks like booking a taxi from the airport and arrive punctually for a meeting demonstrates this.

Belinda's key task is to reinvigorate the team and give them a new direction and strategy. Her approach seems flawed: keep the people who show "any sign of performance." Simply put, if they can send an email, they can keep their job.

Flintstone's choice of pedestrian names for the RSMs (Des, Dave, Ken, Patrick) reflects the mundanity of their jobs and everyday lives. This is further demonstrated in their almost primitive reaction to the "line up of tit" at the Pentra—they clap and chant like cavemen.

The way Flintstone has drawn the dividing lines of each sales manager's area shows no regard for regional borders, and there are some discrepancies between the size of each character's purview. For example, Des Martin is responsible for London and the Home Counties, while Patrick O'Hamlin oversees two entire nations, Scotland and Ireland.

AUTHOR'S NOTE

What was the inspiration for the names of your characters?

I'm constantly asked how I come up with my characters' names and this is so easy to answer; basically I've worked with them all at one time or another. I even used to know a Belinda on the bus going home from school . . . now that's really going back in time! You also have to remember I do spend a fair amount of time outside the UK and I'm continually stumbling across great names, like Sid, to add to my erotic stories.

Rocky x

Reading group discussion points

- Have you ever struggled to get a taxi, and why?

- Discuss Belinda's morale-boosting techniques. Is getting her breasts out an effective strategy to get the best from her team?

- Find the person with the most boring name in your group. How does it match their personality?

- Which RSM do you identify with most, and why?

- Has anyone ever got your name wrong in the same way that Flintstone mistakes Bella for "Donna"? How did it make you feel?

Le Creuset are clearly shitting themselves.

Language Alert

The practice of sporting no undergarments or "inner clothing" [*sic*] is referred to as "going commando."

Certain types of clothes, such as cycling shorts and kilts, are traditionally worn without underpants.

The Maze;

- for me. This has taken forever. Is it really only Chapter 4??

Saturday morning came all too quickly and was bright and breezy, but
dry, ideal for a quick game of tennis and then later a spot of shopping
and browsing through the cook shops of London's Oxford Street. Belinda
thought it was important to not only know her own brand but also those of
the opposition. That evening she planned to do an internet search on the
guest list for tomorrow's function where she would be unable to wear bra or
thong… definitely a strange request.

OK, Nana.

Sunday morning was warm so Belinda put the soft top down and motored
over to Windsor. True to her instructions she checked into the Horse and
Jockey and removed her inner clothing. Now dressed in only her tennis
gear she drove to the Chairman's house. She parked next to Tony's car and
jumped into his passenger seat.

*Mercedes Coupes
don't have soft
tops …
so …*

*Why does everyone inspect everything?
What is he checking for? That they're
good? That there are two?*

Language Alert

Trellis (n) A framework of light wooden or metal bars used to support fruit trees or creepers.

Those of a larger girth could viably accommodate a sales director.

Cultural Context

Police handcuffs are sometimes used in sexual play or BDSM. Use in this context is potentially unwise as they are not specifically designed for this purpose and wearers can suffer from nerve injury or "handcuff neuropathy."

Flintstone preempts readers' concerns by clarifying their toy classification.

'Good morning Tony.' Her tennis skirt had risen up to show the top of her thighs. Tony pulled it up at the front and studied her pussy. He then pulled up her tennis shirt and inspected her tits.

'Hi Belinda, good to see you're good to go, so lets quickly go through the guest list and discuss our targets with their potential. After we've done this we'll get some lunch and take up our positions.

Less sass from you, Blumenthal.   — *Drink!*

'So I can readjust my clothing Tony?' Belinda blinked. 'Or do you want me to parade to lunch like this?'

Forty minutes later after some food and two strong gin and tonics, Tony took her to a medium sized garden maze located at the rear of the property. They entered the tall undergrowth and Tony led her through it without a pause. Belinda was glad someone knew their way through the myriad of paths and openings. After three minutes they entered a glade which was obviously the central point of the maze. He pushed Belinda's back onto a flimsy wooden trellis, gave her a quick kiss and attached her arms to the trellis with a set of red plastic handcuffs attached to a length of parcel string. Belinda was now thoroughly intrigued and a little excited at what was about to happen and laughed out loud, 'Tony, how did you know my favourite handcuff colour was red? Seriously though, I've not seen a pair of these since my days in Kindergarten!'

She's being trussed up like a spatchcock hen!

Who has a favorite handcuff color?

When does anyone ever play with handcuffs at nursery?!

Is this the same as "whetting her appetite"?

It's parcel string and plastic—my ninety-year-old grandma could break free.

Talking Point

Whistling can connote many moods, from ominous in the iconic scene from *Kill Bill* to defiant pride in *The Bridge on the River Kwai*. What mood is Alfonse's whistling intended to create?

Cultural Context

The glades of fairy tales are magical places filled with mythical creatures, from pixies and fawns to centaurs and unicorns.

As a jagged anticlimax, Rocky Flintstone places only Belinda Blumenthal in his.

So creepy.

Tony smiled as he backed away from Belinda.

'Tony... what's going on?' said Belinda now seriously trying to control her amusement.

'Trust me Belinda, treat your clients well and let's see the business roll in. I'll return and "release" you in under two hours. Keep your chin up and let your tits and clit do the talking!' With these erotic words ringing in her ears, Tony walked off. *FUCKING. HELL.*

The grass underfoot felt wet and Belinda could hear a sprinkler nearby which kept wetting her ankles, the area of wet grass would soon become a mud patch she thought... how disgusting. She hated mud at the best of times, but tied to this garden fence meant she couldn't move around... much it would soon get really muddy and quickly.

Those tennis whites are gonna need to go on a hot wash for more than one reason.

Her thoughts were interrupted by the sound of cheerful whistling coming down the maze. Ahh, here's my first client she thought.

Not so much a name as a collection of letters.

Alfonse Stirbacker from Belgium strolled into the glade and studied Belinda's position with obvious interest. From Tony's outline and her internet research, Belinda recognized him and his potential immediately... over 300 supermarket outlets throughout Belgium, Northern France and Southern Holland and they were soon to push into the UK.

'A good start.' she thought.

🖤 CHARACTER PROFILE: Tony

Tony is MD at Steele's Pots and Pans and one of the first characters we meet. His rugged features make him the focus of much sexual attention from the ladies of the office.

His number one key to success is premium meeting spaces, and at great cost to the company he installed a room decked out entirely in leather tiles. He uses this much like a prayer room at an airport—for moments of deep contemplation and seducing his PA.

The stripping of Belinda, his interviewee in Chapter 1, can only lead us to believe that he has scant respect for HR directives. Put simply, he's a renegade with a powerful penchant for breasts and vaginas, in which he often indulges.

- **Physical Attribute:** Rugged features

- **Dominant Character Trait:** Risk-taker

- **Unusual Skill:** Ability to manage Belinda Blumenthal

- **Fun Fact:** Only has sex on leather

♞ ACTIVITY

In this chapter Belinda is liberated by her lack of underwear. Put yourself in her shoes and remove your "inner clothing" for the rest of the day. How does this lack of bra and/or thong make you feel? What are the limitations and benefits?

🔑 KEY THEME: Horticulture, the Greatest Mazes of the World

The maze can be read as a metaphor for Belinda's labyrinthine sex life—a series of dead ends, wrong turns, and bad decisions. Flintstone himself has gone on record to state he found inspiration in the oldest hedge maze in Britain: Hampton Court Maze. Built in 1689 during the time of William III of Orange, several other works of literature over the generations have incorporated its corridors and passages.

However, the world's longest maze is at the Dole Plantation on Oahu, Hawaii, and is made up of nearly 14,000 tropical native plants. Dole has not only created the largest maze on earth; the company also offers a virtual version so you can try your navigation skills from the comfort of your laptop.

Flintstone had the opportunity in this work of fiction to compete and create a magical, never-ending warren of walkways. Instead he opted for an unremarkable "medium-sized maze."

✏️ AUTHOR'S NOTE

Why did you choose to dress Belinda in tennis wear?

All-white tennis wear on a woman is a total turn-on, perhaps that's why I like Wimbledon so much. A crisp white short-sleeved shirt with short shorts is close to a uniform but still not quite that. It makes a statement, shouting, "Watch me, I'm professional—give me the respect I deserve."

Rocky x

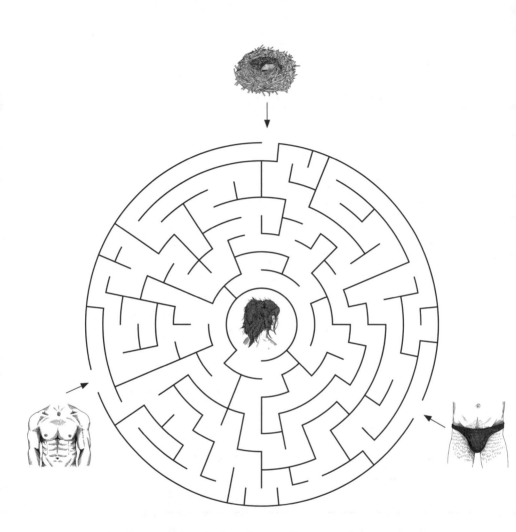

This chapter finds Belinda tied to a trellis in a medium-sized maze.
Help each of the three potential clients find their route to our
horny heroine and her handcuffs.

✎ LANGUAGE ALERT
Vaginal Personification

The "talking vagina" is a significant tradition in literature and art, perhaps most prominent as the central trope of *The Vagina Monologues*. In the "let your tits and clit do the talking" passage of *Belinda Blinked 1*, Flintstone's fascination with this theme is brought to the fore. Belinda herself is essentially a mute, but her clitoris is highly talkative. Another tradition is a vagina that acquires the power of speech to play the role of informant, revealing a lover's previous sexual history. We assume the author has avoided this incarnation, as in the case of Belinda it would require a much longer novel.

📖 Reading group discussion points

- In what setting is it appropriate to study your colleague's pussy?

- Discuss the best ways to track your route through a maze.

- What does your favorite handcuff color say about you?

- There are several health and beauty benefits to mud. List three.

- Have you ever been attached to a piece of garden equipment? What were the emotions connected to the event?

Is she saying this to Alfonse? What's dialogue and what's not? This is chaos.

She is the least enigmatic character ever written.

CHAPTER 5

The First Client; Alfonse Stirbacker

How old is Alfonse?

'Good afternoon young lady, and who do I have the pleasure of meeting, albeit in this strange situation?'

Thank fuck someone is addressing the elephant in the room.

'Hi Mr Stirbacker, my name is Belinda Blumenthal and I'm the Sales Director of Steele Pots and Pans. She always felt she should apologise for the terrible company name, but she also knew it was so awful that very few people ever forgot it.

I wish I could forget this book.

Stirbacker replied, 'Excellent, you look like my type of girl… young, dark and mysterious! As you know my name you will also know I am the purchasing director of my company. Let's get to know each other, we have only 20 minutes contact and I intend to make full use of them.

It's not a prison visit.

Cultural Context

The author is known to have met an "Alfonse" in South America who was from the Belgian Congo. He had lots of money, was really good company, and was a pretty good cook. He never met his wife.

Speculation is rife that he informed the character of Alfonse Stirbacker, whom we meet here in Chapter 5.

Language Alert

Alfonse uses "lady" and "girl" to address Belinda; she uses "gentleman" for him—what does this tell us about their relationship?

Cultural Context

Here Flintstone harks back to the popular "Pool Rules" posters of the 1970s and 1980s, which outlined the sanctions on swimming etiquette.

Controversially, running, ducking, bombing, and shouting were all banned during this era, but it was the clamping down on "heavy petting" that Flintstone never forgot.

Language Alert

People often confuse the vulva with the vagina. The vagina, also known as the birth canal, is internal. The vulva, however, consists of the external genital organs of a woman. It is quite possible Flintstone believes these terms can be used interchangeably.

Alfonse immediately got to work by removing his one garment of a black thong and taking off Belinda's shoes and socks. Completely naked he pushed up her white shirt partially uncovering her breasts. He then pulled her tennis skirt down to her knees and backed off. How strange Belinda thought… he's just a voyeur… he doesn't want any close contact. Maybe he's happily married?

How HAPPILY married are you if you're willing to fuck a stranger in a maze?

I think what's about to happen is disgusting— let's not blame the environment.

Alfonse then said to Belinda, 'Would you visit me in my offices in Brussels and let me see your body again? Perhaps I could see more of it, and possibly in a less disgusting environment. Belinda immediately understood, Alfonse needed order and homely comforts in order to progress his male desires, though his cock had quickly become completely erect. She replied, 'Absolutely Mr Stirbacker I'm so glad I fit your expectations, and I would really like to do a lot of business with you

Why do I think this has nothing to do with pots and pans?

Her tits are at a bus stop.

Stirbacker grinned and said, 'That is assured my lovely Belinda, and he fondled her waiting tits with relish. Belinda groaned softly, one of his hands slipped down to her vagina and started to gently caress it. In return she stroked his penis with both hands

I just can't get the idea of him slathering her with piccalilli out of my head.

Hang on, her hands are tied to the trellis. Is she Debbie McGee?

'A gentleman from Brussels thought Belinda, what a great start to the afternoon!' After a further ten minutes of extremely heavy fondling, Belinda was becoming very wet, Alfonse had now gotten to her tits big time with his teeth and his very long cock had penetrated her vulva. He was obviously

I notice he hasn't put "big"; he's chosen "long." Is it like a Slim Jim?

That is the weirdest
euphemism for an orgasm I've
ever heard.

Never have I been
so relieved to hear
any sound ever in my
whole life.

How would anyone know if she
has her thong on or not?! It's
UNDER her clothes.

Is she ever living in the moment? CONCENTRATE.

enjoying her tits and clit as Tony had put it so aptly just fifteen minutes earlier, and she had her first major client breakthrough. She mentally penciled in a visit to Brussels in ten days time. No sense in not striking whilst the iron was hot… so to speak!

Like a wounded animal.

A far off whistle sounded and Alfonse backed off.. 'Time for me to go Belinda, I thoroughly enjoyed your lack of bra and thong… very thoughtful, but don't forget them when you visit me in Brussels very soon. We will have dinner at my very exclusive gentleman's club and all our ladies are expected to be properly dressed… at least when they arrive!

Belinda replied, 'Don't worry Mr Stirbacker I'll be in touch very soon!

You can't shut her up in this chapter.

I beg to differ. It's really thoughtful to send flowers or a thank-you card, not to whip off your knickers.

⦿ CHARACTER PROFILE: Alfonse Stirbacker

Alfonse Stirbacker of Brussels is impressive to Belinda thanks to his three-hundred-strong fleet of supermarket outlets throughout Belgium, northern France, and southern Holland. She likes that he is a powerful businessman who clearly understands the market. But it's not just his corporate acumen that she's attracted to; he has a very long cock—almost two hands' worth.

Alfonse is a mover and a shaker in the world of pots and pans—an award-winning entrepreneur, he enjoys the finer things in life. To give us an idea of his status, Flintstone lets us know that he is a member of a very exclusive gentlemen's club.

Belinda and Alfonse are somewhat kindred spirits in terms of approach, mixing business and pleasure effortlessly. Though sometimes mistaken for just a voyeur, Stirbacker can be seen chatting through meeting arrangements mid-intercourse. He is not afraid to wear his sexuality on his sleeve, happily sporting a black thong.

• **Physical Attribute:** Has never been seen without a black thong

• **Dominant Character Trait:** Belgian

• **Unusual Skill:** Voyeurism

• **Fun Fact:** Responds adversely to whistles

⦿ ACTIVITY

Belinda and Alfonse only had "twenty minutes contact." In pairs, see how much you can learn about each other in the same amount of time, using only your hands and faces.

(Q) KEY THEME: Belgium

Stirbacker originating from Belgium is no arbitrary detail. The country was chosen for its rich and varied history. It's not just the land of waffles and pralines, but a hub of creativity and business know-how. Famously, Belgian physicist and mathematician Ingrid Daubechies developed the model used by the FBI to record fingerprints. But perhaps more notably, Belgians are the most avid users of discount coupons in the world.

(✎) AUTHOR'S NOTE

Why did you choose thongs for the men?

Brazil, where I spend half the year, is just full of men in thongs. Never mind the ladies, you even see ninety-year-old grannies wearing them. I think men look good in thongs; you avoid that tiresome white tan mark around your backside, and they do look sexy. It can be a liberating experience wearing a thong, but not every male will dare to do it.

Rocky x

(📖) Reading group discussion points

- In a group, discuss how disgusting it is to see a man wearing a thong. What adjectives could describe your repulsion?

- Have you ever visited Belgium? Discuss the worst elements of the trip.

- What are the pros and cons of securing a business deal through sex?

What? Smooth like
an Action Man? ————

If you don't see it straight away ————
there's a concern.

CHAPTER 6

The Second Client; Jim Stirling

Is it a T. rex?

A few minutes after Alfonse had gone Belinda heard her second visitor stomping through the maze. He appeared a few seconds later, again dressed only in a black thong. It was becoming a type of uniform she thought. From the guest list info Belinda recognized Jim Stirling, a Yankee from the USA. His operation had 1257 outlets and was also growing fast in Mexico and Brazil. He was a big guy but short, and upon seeing Belinda's plight quickly threw his somewhat stained thong to the ground.

Drink!

Belinda blinked;   *WHAT IS IT STAINED WITH?????!!!*

For the first time that day she was caught unawares... there was nothing there, but then she saw it, underneath covered in pubic hairs lay a very   *GAG.*
small and in Belinda terms, somewhat pathetic penis, Belinda gasped, what
was she expected to do with this?   *Why? Is it curled up in its nest
like a small woodland creature?*

It's a vole. His penis is a vole.

No one is turned on by the word "squatted."

Jim's penis is an apparition and it's haunting Belinda's vagina.

We need backup—get the thumbs!

'Hi, my name's Stirling, from the US. Let's get these garments out of the way!'

With one powerful movement he ripped Belinda's tennis shirt completely from her body, and seconds later had done the same to her skirt. He flung them to the ground where they now lay ruined in the mud. *Poor bastard—he's got huge everything, but a tiny dick.*

'Hope you don't mind Missy as I likes 'em bare!' Jim didn't hang around and immediately took her tits in his massive hands. His large thumbs tentatively rubbed her nipple tips, making them rise and harden. This fast reaction from Belinda seemed to please him and he started to push his cock into her vagina. *You have to ask yourself some big questions when your thumbs are the most erotic thing about you.*

Belinda squatted slightly as Jim was shorter than her, pulling her legs apart to allow him easier access. Jim grunted and Belinda thought she felt something entering her pussy. He started to fuck her hard, Belinda breathed deeply, did the man know he was only tickling her? This was going to take all her concentration, Stirling's was a massive account and if she did well today, who knew what might develop from it. He started to press her harder and harder against the trellis, he had found his rhythm but Belinda couldn't feel anything and whilst she had the appetite for it she knew she would have to fake it and Belinda never faked anything. To make matters worse the ground was now really boggy and her torn garments were well and truly stained.

Why is there a rogue comma? Is that Jim's penis? To scale?

Ironic.

This sounds like a cable TV legal advert. "Have YOU got the friction you need to complete your ejaculation? If not, why not? Call 0800 GET WOOD to make a claim."

The only work she's done in this entire book.

Cultural Context

Notable aphrodisiacs include oysters, chocolate, and Flintstone's favorite fruit, the pomegranate.

Runny, barely cooked eggs are a food less commonly associated with sex.

Great time for introductions, Jim. Priorities.

Basically anything but this.

Belinda thought of delicious sexual scenarios and succeeded in making her vagina become wetter and wetter. She started to slowly contract her cervical muscles to ensure Jim got the friction he needed to complete his ejaculation. After ten minutes of hard work he came and then started to lick her tits. He obviously had little regard for women as he then pushed her head down to his cock ensuring Belinda's long black hair fell nearly to the by now muddy ground, her ample breasts followed and Stirling pushed his penis into her mouth. Belinda smiled to herself, she could have eaten two of these for breakfast, never mind the scrambled eggs. *Are they on a time delay?*

Just then she heard the whistle and she knew she had done her best. Stirling reluctantly let go of her tits and put his thong back on… it was now even more stained than when he had entered the maze and Belinda wondered where all the semen had come from. Perhaps she had underestimated his resources? *Mighty cum from little acorn's gush.* *"A" for effort.*

'Hey babe, what's your name?' said Stirling.

'Belinda Blumenthal, I'm the Sales Director of Steele Pots and Pans.'

'Good work Belinda, come and see me in Texas in a couple of weeks… I need a new cookery utensil supplier and I guess you fit the bill!

*I imagine Belinda dressed up as a cowgirl, doing the cowgirl sex position. *Shudder**

'Why Jim, I'd love to… let's say in three weeks time?

'Yup… let's do it… and I promise to replace your soiled garments with something a little bit more sexy! — *People in stained thongs shouldn't throw stones.*

With that he stumped off leaving Belinda completely naked, very muddy and still tied to the trellis around the maze. She massaged her wrists where the red plastic handcuffs had managed to keep her attached to the trellis and thought of the bonus money she would personally make when she tied up the deal with Jim Stirling. She also thought she should take a crash course in Yoga, or some sort of exercises which developed the cervix muscles. If Jim couldn't rise to the job then she would have to ensure he was completely satisfied… the things she did to make her fortune! — *I think I'd rather be on the breadline.*

Jesus, ANOTHER one?!

But wait, she could hear another client approaching through the maze. 'Oh no,' she thought, 'I hope this one's a bit better hung, I can't take much more of these small appendages.' But she had to… the handcuffs and parcel string ensured it!

Amen.

Oh yeah, the kids' toy and some twine. It's a proper Fort Knox.

CHARACTER PROFILE: Jim Stirling

Jim Stirling is an Austin-based, Dallas-born American who is proficient in business, who oversees a massive account of 1,257 cookware outlets. His entrepreneurial flare is so strong that his organization is growing fast in the markets of Mexico and Brazil, despite both nations being in recession (at the time of publication).

Not a man known for his good looks, Jim is blessed with size in every area except one. Fat and with massive hands but a tiny penis, he would have plenty of cause to shy away from intimate relations with the opposite sex. However, Jim is as body confident as a man twice his height and double his girth.

Despite his "pathetic" penis being dubbed "the vole" in popular culture, his incessant grunting during intercourse, and being the subject of the revisionist nursery rhyme—"I'm Jim Stirling, short and stout, here's my handle, where's my spout?"—Stirling is a content crooner and the perfect foil for Belinda.

• **Physical Attribute:** Huge thumbs

• **Dominant Character Trait:** Brash

• **Unusual Skill:** His penis can pass as a vole in a hole

• **Fun Fact:** From the same state as Beyoncé

⊙ KEY THEME: The Male Body

Jim Stirling appears to possess what has long been believed to be a mythical organ dubbed "the chode."

A chode is purported to be a penis that is wider than it is long. Debate rages as to whether such a thing exists in reality, though the plight of the "micropenis" was examined on popular daytime talk show *This Morning* in January 2016.

The desirable size of the male human's penis has shifted throughout history. Kenneth Dover's landmark study *Greek Homosexuality* concluded that in ancient Greece a small penis was culturally seen as desirable.

However, in subsequent centuries a large penis has been viewed as a symbol of strength and power. It is therefore notable that Flintstone has chosen to depict Stirling with a "very small" and "somewhat pathetic" endowment.

✒ AUTHOR'S NOTE

Why did you make Jim Stirling a micro-genitaled American?

This chapter took a couple of rewrites to get the correct feeling—Jim was initially going to be French, but I thought the French as a nation wouldn't be able to see the funny side of the scenario. The only nation in the world whom I thought could take it was the good ole USA . . . I've done business with Americans many times; I've even worked for them, and I've always found them great fun and they love a beer. I'm not so keen on their style of gin and tonic, which they call a Tom Collins . . . but, hey . . . it's still alcohol!

The fact that Jim is not over-endowed like many men, if truth be told, was important in bringing a bit of surprise and variety into the maze scenes.

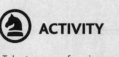

Rocky x

♞ ACTIVITY

Take turns performing your best "fake orgasm."

 **Reading group discussion points**

- Debate whether Rocky is making a social comment against the "bigger is better" adage in relation to the male sexual organ.

- Belinda is nothing if not determined and goes to extraordinary lengths to secure a business deal. What is the most extreme thing you have done to get what you want?

- What substance do you think Jim's thong is stained with? What clues does the text provide?

Cultural Context—Bowing

Bowing is most prominent in Asian cultures or typical of nobility and aristocracy in Europe. Peter is neither Asian nor an aristocrat.

CHAPTER 7

The Third Client; Peter Rouse

Not easy in that quagmire.

Belinda stood her ground hoping this one would be so much better, she had had enough titillation, she wanted, no, needed a good fuck. A tall blonde haired man, with an impressive physique strolled into view. Belinda quickly recognised Peter Rouse, his operation was located in Holland with 357 retail outlets, and again was growing strongly throughout the Scandinavian countries. An evasive entrepreneur, Peter could not be overlooked as he had recently expanded to Spain and Portugal. On seeing Belinda he quickly removed his thong and threw it to the ground whilst approaching her.

The spiritual home of pots and pans.

Imagine having that effect on someone. As soon as they see you, they whip their pants off.

'My name is Peter,' he said and quickly bowed, 'I believe you are Belinda, the Sales Director of this fantastic customer bash your superiors are putting on here today!'

What year is Peter from? Has this become a Jane Austen novel?

Language Alert

This dialogue invokes a similar phrase to that of the fairy tale "Little Red Riding Hood," a story that has been interpreted as a metaphor for sexual awakening. The red cloak symbolizes the blood of menstruation, the wolf symbolizes her lover, and to reach her destination she must brave the "dark forest" of womanhood.

He's gone for the fail-safe neck, boobs, bum maneuver.

Two uses of "body." We know you have a thesaurus, Dad, no excuses.

You get a lot of vagina to the pound in this book. At least it's value for money.

Now she blushes …

'Why yes I am Mr. Rouse.' said Belinda, blushing at her naked appearance in front of this, so far, delightfully hung man. After all, he was the first to know who she was. *He knows your name?! If that's not a reason to shag someone, I don't know what is.*

'Please, please call me Peter,' he replied, 'especially as we are to become more intimately acquainted in the next 25 minutes.' He took Belinda's hands and said, 'What a delightful body you have, may I handle it?' *It's not a fragile item.*

Belinda replied, 'Why yes of course… I would love to feel you touch me, feel as free as you wish.'

'Now that's an offer I cannot refuse,' Peter replied and immediately started to massage her neck, slowly spreading to her breasts and buttocks. Belinda immediately started to relax and responded by gently massaging Peter's penis. *Kinda sounds like she's kneading it like dough, like an uncooked baguette.*

He had a fantastic body and his muscles were very well toned, Belinda started to caress his body and in return he moved his massage to her vaginal area. He stroked her small runway of pubic black hair leading to her vaginal lips, and soon he was inside her with his fingers Belinda had rarely experienced anything as delicate as this and soon began to moan softly. In return she still had the sense of presence to massage his now extremely hard and large penis. She somehow knew she was going to enjoy this man. *How many fingers? What's he doing in there? Playing rock-paper-scissors? Cat's cradle?*

Does not sound delicate.

I think Belinda
might die in this
chapter.

Via the mouth?!
With his penis??!

What's wrong with just saying, "They had sex"?

Is she exfoliating him?

She's as mad as a box of frogs!

After a few moments Peter pushed Belinda onto her knees, into the soft
mud and gently guided her head to his penis. Belinda opened her mouth
and slowly pushed her lips over his foreskin, pulling it back before slightly
gagging as she swallowed his entire cock down her throat 'You are very
skilful Belinda, would you let me teach you more techniques?'

Aaaaaand vomit.

'Why yes Peter I always love to learn new things.'

How's she answering? Her mouth is definitely full.

He then lifted her from the ground and slowly penetrated her vagina with
his now throbbing cock. Belinda again moaned softly…his penetration was
so fluid she felt in ecstasy. He started to move inside her, she responded by
contracting and releasing her vaginal muscles in time to his thrusts. They
were now completely intertwined, Belinda had never experienced anything
like this before, she was floating on air and Peter was penetrating deeper
and deeper. Belinda started to gasp in short spasms, she needed more and
more oxygen just to feed the gigantic orgasm she was about to encounter.
For the first time in her life she was not in control, but she was enjoying it to
death.

What? Actual normal sex? With a nice polite man?

Peter started to sweat profusely, Belinda started to rub his skin more
vigorously and he approached his climax. Of course Belinda was now wild
with delirium, she was completely out of her head, all her actions were
mechanical, Peter kept thrusting, Belinda kept flexing her vaginal
muscles, until they both came in a violent explosion of ecstasy together.

Give it a minute, Belinda! That
was barely a pit stop.

TEETH!?!?!?!

Wasn't her first thought "girlfriend"
rather than "sex slave"?

How big are her lobes that he
can draw on them?

m picturing him plopping
t of the end of the flume
- the local swimming pool.

Are they actually
sinking now?

Peter fell out of her. Belinda collapsed onto her knees in the mud… the
plastic handcuffs around her wrists saving her from being completely
immersed. Now on her knees she was spattered all over with the horrible
slime, and there was nothing she could do about it… except linger in the
fantastic orgasm she had just experienced.

But Peter's cock remained erect and Belinda was so impressed with his
skills, she knew she could learn much more from him. So she crawled back
to him and put her mouth over his penis and continued to screw him with
her lips, teeth, tongue and throat… she secretly knew she was ready to
become his sex slave if he would ask her. She would scream for more until
he agreed she thought.

That wouldn't be annoying at all.

But Peter Rouse was no normal individual and he knew when a girl was
under his sexual spell as Belinda now was, so he let her screw his penis in
her mouth and began using the mud to mark Belinda's tits, ass, mouth, and
ears with symbolic signs. She was still kneeling on the ground so he took
the opportunity to write more symbols on her back which would bind her
to him sexually for the next year.

Is he Spider-Man?

His cock then started to ejaculate semen which he quickly caught in his
hands. He then covered her hair with it, twisting it all into a ponytail,
Belinda's long black hair mixed with translucent sperm… the most powerful
sexual symbol he knew. Belinda, though she didn't know it, was now well

I'm never
borrowing my
dad's Brylcreem
again…

Said no one ever. ——————————

Weirdest wedding vows I've ever heard. ——————————

and truly ensnared, though truth be told it was what Belinda would have
wanted.   *Is the maze a time machine?*

*Definitely clear
up the mud
before the cum.*

The whistle brought them both back to the present day. Peter hurriedly
put on his thong whilst Belinda tried to get rid of some of the mud she was
now covered in. Belinda gasped, 'When can I see you next Peter…. please.'
she said desperately. 'Hush my beautiful Belinda, I will see you tonight at
11.30pm in the Horse and Jockey pub, where I know you have a room we
can use.' Belinda smiled her gratitude to him and said, 'It will be so good… I
promise you… ask anything you want… I somehow feel enslaved to you.'

'You are Belinda, as I am to you.' replied Peter. 'Until tonight!'

⊕ CHARACTER PROFILE: Peter Rouse

Peter Rouse is a tall blond man from Amsterdam, Holland. He currently manages 357 retail outlets and that number is growing quickly throughout Scandinavia. Peter is notoriously hard to pin down for a meeting, so to have him in the maze is a real career coup for Belinda. With a toned, sculpted physique, a confident demeanor, and a large penis (uncircumcised), Peter is clearly a hit with the ladies and Belinda is instantly drawn to him. He appears to be a very experienced lover. Early speculation suggests Peter is the first real romantic interest for Belinda.

Sexually, Peter observes some unusual customs; he bows to greet people, he draws symbols in mud all over Belinda's body, and he rubs his semen all over her hair. The sources of these affectations are never explained.

• **Physical Attribute:** Golden haired

• **Dominant Character Trait:** Overly formal—bows on greeting

• **Unusual Skill:** Fluent in ancient languages

• **Fun Fact:** He's happily married

ⓠ KEY THEME: Ancient Iconography

Peter's interest in symbolism is revealed early on. Flintstone has stated that Peter is a very religious man and a member of a secret sect who only worship at midnight. What is clear is that they use a series of markings to tie future sacrifices to them mentally; whether this is a romantic gesture or misogynistic territory-marking is open to interpretation.

✎ AUTHOR'S NOTE

It feels like there's a burgeoning romance between Peter and Belinda. Was this intentional?

Belinda was in a rebound period after Jim Stirling. This left her open to a deeper emotional connection. Basically she was feeling a bit let down and then Peter arrived in the maze. It was inevitable sparks would fly. Whatever happens romantically, Belinda has locked in a key player in the European pots-and-pans distribution field. Put it this way: the future is bright for both of these characters.

Visual guide to Peter Rouse's mud ritual

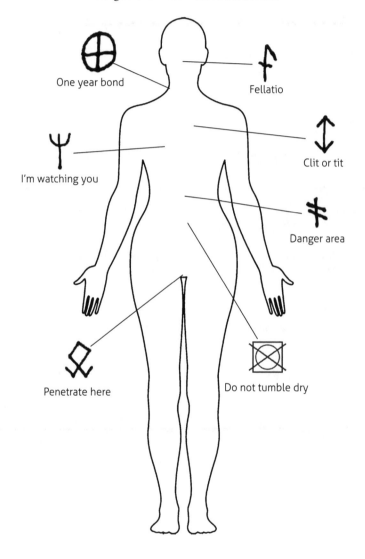

One year bond

Fellatio

I'm watching you

Clit or tit

Danger area

Penetrate here

Do not tumble dry

Reading group discussion points

- What do you think of Belinda and Peter's relationship? Could you see them getting married?

- Discuss the weirdest sexual encounter you've ever had.

- Apart from penis size, in what ways is Peter Rouse different from Jim Stirling, Belinda's previous maze encounter?

- We are now at the halfway point of the book. How much of your life do you feel like you have wasted?

Language Alert

Alliteration is a common literary device, with schoolchildren able to command it from the age of ten.

It's starting to sound a bit like a David Attenborough program: "The male approaches the female with a black thong."

Cultural Context

The "sixth sense" is a supposed intuition giving awareness not explicable by normal forms of perception. In the novel this replaces Belinda's "common sense" so in theory she's back to five.

How strong is Belinda? She's the female Hulk.

Chapter 8

The Tombola (Lottery);

Harsh... but fair. Two and a vole.

Belinda was now both exhausted and exhilarated, she had been fucked by three males... well let's be honest... two and a half in the last two hours and had been totally mesmerized by one of them. She also had a sixth sense that she could never opt out of the special relationship Peter Rouse and herself had developed in their short meeting. But for all that she was completely up for it, Peter was a successful, dominating character... and come to think of it, so was she.

He's Blair and she's Bush. So to speak.

Quite the spa weekend.

Now relaxing against the trellis she pulled the parcel string sharply and it fell to the muddy ground. She slowly twisted the plastic handcuffs, they fell apart and she bent down to pick up her tennis outfit. It was a real mess, but for decency's sake she put what was left of the shirt and dress back on. She knew Tony would be here any minute to bring her back to the BBQ area and then she could get back to her lovely bath at her room in the Horse and Jockey.

There'll be only a cold sausage left by now.

She might need two dips. (One medicated.)

*Can we just see the job
spec one more time?* ⎯⎯⎯

Soon she heard footsteps coming through the maze and thankfully it was

Tony, he had a large smile on his face.

Entertained? She didn't make them balloon animals.

'You're a star Belinda, those three guys you just entertained are over the

moon with you… and the other girls have done good as well.'

'What do you mean other girls?'

'Didn't you know? Giselle and Bella are here as well, it's not just you… it's

your glee team as well!'

Even his own characters are confused.

'Tony! What do you mean by 'glee team'' we're all just girls out for a good

time and I need a bath!'

Yes, we know.

As it's mainly his fault, probably best to keep schtum.

Tony looked at her and decided not to comment on her condition…he had

never seen so much mud stick to a person and what were those symbolic

marks on her face and thighs? *And ears. Don't forget the ears.*

They soon reached the BBQ area which had been transformed into a

Roman-style amphitheater with over 40 people sitting around on chairs.

They were mostly clients with their wives who had up to this point no

knowledge of the sexual adventures which a few of their number had been

allowed access to. Belinda sat down on a chair which Tony had found for

her. She looked around and tried to locate Giselle and Bella.

Sooooo many people are getting divorced tomorrow.

Where did they get all these safety pins from? Is there a haberdashery in the maze?

Does this feel like an appropriate time to be playing games from a school fete?

Belinda gasped when she recognised Giselle, her beautiful blonde hair had been, to say the best, remodeled, by perhaps a maniac with a twist for the dramatic??? Her dress had seen as much wear as Belinda's tennis outfit and was being held together by a few safety pins. Giselle looked up and saw Belinda staring at her, she smiled and stared back at Belinda's equally disgusting condition and torn clothing. Belinda thought perhaps she had gotten off lightly, but why was Tony so happy, Giselle was his girl and she seemed to be in a bit of a state. Belinda gave Giselle the thumbs up and looked around for Bella.

Giselle's like "bitch stole my look."

She soon spotted her and to be honest Bella didn't look that much better than Giselle, though her hair was intact, her outfit was sporting half a dozen safety pins. Bella's face was however covered in red lipstick as though another maniac had tried to apply it. They had definitely succeeded in making her look like a tart. Belinda caught Bella's eye and smiled at her. Bella gave her the thumbs up and smiled back.

Is Giselle bald????

Who invited all the maniacs?

Will everyone stop doing this—they're clearly not OK

Belinda thought, 'This is very strange, what's going to happen next?'

We're literally five steps ahead of you.

A couple of minutes later a tall chap stood up and addressed the gathering.

'Welcome everyone to our annual Tombola where our prizes are the same as previous years. I also want to personally thank Sir James Godwin for letting us have this opportunity to raise some much needed money for our local

Yeah, Dad. But as this is fictitious can you just tell us?

This guy's going to be gold.

What, some hand lotion and a bath bomb?

You win a human being??

No name. Why waste time on detail?

> **Cultural Context**
>
> With his "there is also only one rule [of the tombola]" speech, Flintstone is making a shrewd reference to David Fincher's cult film, *Fight Club*:
>
> "The first rule of Fight Club is: you do not talk about Fight Club. The second rule of Fight Club is: you DO NOT talk about Fight Club!"

I imagine this said very quickly like the small print on a radio ad.

THIMBLE THIMBLE THIMBLE THIMBLE THIMBLE THIMBLE THIMBLE THIMBLE.

What sort of charity is endorsing this form of fund-raising?

What kind of asses are we talking here?

charity, The Asses & Donkeys Trust. Now, please remember as your prize is a real person you will only get your servant for the time period of 12 hours. The highest bidder from this audience for each individual prize gets to take them home!' The audience clapped enthusiastically.

Feel like this might be the longest half-day of all our lives.

The tall man continued, 'There is also only one rule, and that is we have a safe word, which when uttered means the owner stops the directed task right away and the servant is released from their 12 hour duty. The down side of that is, the servant has to match the donation paid by the bidder to our charity! We all win! OK! Yes, now please remember girls and potential owners the safe word is THIMBLE, yes thimble… easy to remember, it stops you from getting pricked!! Ha ha!' The crowd groaned and started clapping.

Drink!

Bravo! Lovely joke from the Tall Man.

Tough crowd.

Belinda blinked; she was intrigued, this sounds like great fun. She quickly thought, 'Who would I pick as my prize… Tony?… Bella?… no, Sir James Godwin and boy would I enjoy that scenario.'

Really?!

Based on nothing.

'Today we have three servants on offer and to find out who they are, and take note it could be any one of you here, I want you all to look under your chairs and see the number attached to it.' The sound of hurriedly scraping chairs filled the air whilst the now hushed audience checked their numbers. Belinda's was 13, 'Unlucky for some,' she thought.

Spoiler; and you.

Even the wives who thought they were off to Ascot?

Surprise fucking surprise #1. _____

Surprise fucking surprise #2.

Cultural Context

There is a great importance and relevance to the numbers selected in the tombola: 22, 37, and, finally, 13.

Traditional tarot decks have twenty-two cards; the number thirty-seven is used four times in the Bible; and thirteen is the nickname of Dr. Remy Hadley in the medical drama *House*.

Can you have a receding pubic hairline / _____
a pubic widow's peak / a pubic cowlick?

THE TOMBOLA (LOTTERY);

I've been to a lot of tombolas in my time. And no one has ever said that.

'Ok,' the tall man shouted, 'let's tumble the tombola and see what the three "lucky" numbers are.' The tombola went round and round, Belinda felt a sense of adventure take over her persona, she somehow felt she knew she would be a prize, but she didn't know who would be her owner.

What's the number again?

'The first number is 22, I repeat 22, would the person sitting on chair number 22 please stand up.' Belinda looked around to see who the lucky person was. It was Giselle and as she stood up a safety pin fell out revealing a beautiful right breast to the crowd. An appreciative murmur came from the men, which saw many of their wives elbowing them in the ribs. Did they dare bid for her after that Belinda thought?

If they're getting pissed off now, wait till the bidding starts.

'The second number is 37, I repeat 37.'

Bella stood up, her safety pins held and Belinda started to smell a rat.

'The third number is, unlucky for some, 13, I repeat number 13.'

Belinda jumped to her feet, ready to go, wondering who she would be a servant to for the next twelve hours. Her torn shirt fell wide apart revealing her breasts and her tennis skirt flapped wide in the mounting breeze *THIMBLE.* revealing her pubic hairline to the assembled body, but she didn't care, she was Belinda and she was going to make sure a big butch man took her home!

Why's she talking in the third person?

Best of luck, chuck.

101

Gutted. Talk about short straw. Literally.

What's wrong with a sponsored bike ride?

'Now,' said the tall man, 'This is where we make some money for our charity as the rest of you can bid for their services, but firstly, do I have the agreement of these three very fine ladies to be coerced into these important roles?'

Belinda thought, 'What the fuck, this might be fun… it's probably just doing a bit of cleaning and lawn mowing on a Sunday evening.'

OF COURSE IT'S NOT.

She shouted out, 'Yes I'm game!' whilst covering up her private parts with her hands and arms.

Never have been, never will be, private.

The other two girls followed suit and happily agreed, the tall man bowed to them.

Is the Tall Man Japanese?

'Thank you for your noble assistance, our charity The Asses & Donkeys Trust is much indebted to you.' he said.

The bidding quickly started with Bella and she soon went for £350 to the American Jim Stirling who Belinda thought could do with a cock transplant, and very soon at that. Giselle went next for £300 from Tony of all people, definitely a case of protecting his own. Then it was Belinda's turn. The bids started slowly, and Belinda couldn't believe her body was that bad… perhaps it was all the mud… where was her butch man? Finally

FIX!!!!

This is why the rest of the country is having a hosepipe ban!

I would say how undignified but I think we all know it's completely necessary.

To get into all those nooks and crannies.

Cultural Context

WWI's frugality drive was embodied by the mantra "waste not, want not," which featured on public advice propaganda posters, educating citizens on how to be more resourceful.

The Duchess likely remembers these from her early teens and lives her life by this philosophy today.

It's the man from Del Monte!

— A cool £16 an hour.

she went for £200 from a lady dressed in a <u>white linen trouser suit and a</u> <u>panama hat</u> called only the Duchess.

With Belinda sold, the tombola was over and the three girls were taken away to start their twelve hours of duty. The now devastated Belinda was immediately led to a hosepipe near the stables where the Duchess striped her of her torn skirt and tennis shirt and hosed her down. She roughly fondled Belinda's tits and ass in the washing process with a <u>long handled</u> <u>brush</u> and then pushed her, still naked, into a horsebox. With the rear tail gate down it was obvious that it all had been planned in advance, instead of straw and manure there was a sofa and drinks, albeit chilled, tinned Gin and Tonics.

Why, because she went for the least cash?

Now there's a curveball.

Money can't buy you manners.

The Duchess rudely pushed Belinda onto the sofa and offered her a drink. Belinda nervously poured the can down her by now parched throat, she was still feeling horny and didn't think her new owner could give her what she still craved even after the afternoons events. Quite a lot of the can didn't get down Belinda's throat and she made sure the liquid trickled down her neck onto her breasts and then into her tummy button where it pooled, overflowed and ran down her track of black pubic hair into her vagina.

Why not?

Vagina & tonic!!!

Much to Belinda's surprise the Duchess murmured, 'Waste not, want not,' and promptly licked the gin off Belinda's tits, stomach and clitoris.

Again with the manners. At least
use a straw. ——————

Probably best. ——————

Belinda would love that—can she
trade in the Duchess?
——————

Number three already!
She's going to be wasted.

Cultural Context

A motel is a hotel designed for motorists, which came to prominence in the
1920s as long-distance road journeys became more common.

They are traditionally an inexpensive and "no frills" alternative to hotels,
which poses questions as to why a woman of the Duchess's means would
frequent such an establishment.

Belinda thought "Result!' but said nothing and let the Duchess enjoy her slurping hoping this was setting the tone for the rest of the evening. She asked for another G&T and this time the Duchess decided to pour it down Belinda's throat herself. It was obvious the Duchess was enjoying this relationship, as she cupped her free hand around Belinda's left breast whilst carelessly slopping the drink into her mouth.

A niche choice.

'Had enough servant?' said the Duchess, 'as we have to move on or Sir James will be joining our little party!' The Duchess efficiently closed the tail door of the horse trailer to the chagrin of the quickly assembled party of stable lads, leaving Belinda reclining on the sofa and helping herself to another Gin and Tonic in comfort. It was just as well she could stretch out because the Duchess was not a competent driver of the large four wheel drive vehicle plus trailer. Belinda lost count of the cut corners and sudden halts as they drove through the country lanes to an exclusive Motel which had some private chalets in the grounds. Belinda wickedly hoped the Duchess was better at fucking than driving... or had a companion who could do both.

Wouldn't be difficult from the sound of it.

AUTHOR'S NOTE
What is the personal significance of the tombola?

I used to do a lot for charity when the kids were at junior school, and I invariably ended up running the tombola stall. This was great fun; I loved spinning the ticket container so it was a no-brainer to add this experience into a gloriously English occasion and to add three beautiful girls as willing prizes.

Having the wives at the tombola comes directly from my experiences in selling stuff to customers. I personally don't subscribe to the "day on the golf course" technique where only males attend. I, like Tony and Sir James, much prefer to have a day out with the wife or partner. It also makes good business sense; you get to know the clients' other halves and what pushes their buttons.

Rocky x

✏ CULTURAL CONTEXT

History of Gin and Tonic

Gin and tonics are the favored tipple of the cast of characters of *Belinda Blinked 1*. According to some reports tonic water was first enjoyed in 1825 when British officers in the Indian army improved their bitter anti-malaria medicine—Peruvian quinine extract—by mixing it with soda and sugar. At some point during this time the daily dose of protective quinine tonic was combined with a shot of gin ration, adding lime to fend off scurvy. Winston Churchill is reputed to have said, "The gin and tonic has saved more Englishmen's lives, and minds, than all the doctors in the Empire." Rocky Flintstone has been known to enjoy one or two while he writes in his pavilion, though he prefers new world wines.

Asses and Donkeys Trust (ADT)

Our mission: to transform the quality of life for donkeys and asses across the globe and to ensure their contribution to humankind is fully valued.

Our dream: a world where donkeys and asses live free from cruelty and suffering.

Case study: *Alan the Ass was left abandoned by the side of the M25 with no food or shelter. His owner said he'd be 'right back' but never returned. Alan didn't trust humans and was very nervous when we first met him, but now he averages thirty rides a day on Skegness beach.*

Sponsor Alan today and receive a signed photograph, monthly correspondence and a knitted toy that looks just like him.*

*scaled down

Registered charity no. 7312861864814821 54761481

110

⬛ ACTIVITY

Using only household balms and creams, style a friend's hair into a "maniac" updo. Wear the look out of the house and document the reactions you receive.

📖 Reading group discussion points

- How important is female friendship in this chapter?

- What would someone feel like after having sex with two-and-a-half men?

- What are the main adversities facing modern-day asses and donkeys?

- How much would it cost to convert a traditional horse box into a modern sex cart?

- How bad are women drivers? Why?

Cultural Context—Horse box

It is illegal to have a human being in a horse box without a seat belt. Furthermore, it is illegal to drive under the influence of alcohol. Cumulatively the Duchess could face six months in prison, a driving ban, and thousands of pounds in fines.

Cultural Context—Jilly Cooper

A key influence for Flintstone seems to be romantic novelist Jilly Cooper and her best-known work, *Riders*, set in the competitive world of show jumping. There are comparisons to be made between Flintstone and Cooper. Both authors draw heavily on their own point of view and experiences. Cooper's love of dogs and horses features prominently in her work, whereas Flintstone's passion for breasts and gin and tonic are key themes of his writing.

Is this like the Leather Room?

CHAPTER 9;

The Chalet;

Bless! It's like when you leave a dog in the car. Make sure you crack a window for Belinda!

Belinda felt the horse box reversing accompanied with the grinding of gears and then the engine of the four by four went dead. There was a silence for at least thirty minutes and Belinda started to feel abandoned. Then suddenly the tail gate opened and the Duchess climbed up the ramp. She was dressed in full horse riding gear, a red jacket, white jodhpurs, black boots, black jumping hat and crop with a scarlet tag on the end. Belinda blinked fearing the worst.

— Drink!

The Duchess grabbed Belinda's ass and pulled her up to a standing position. She then pushed her down the ramp and pulled her by her left tit into a chalet style building. The Duchess made for a doorway at the end of the lounge which led to a large wet room. She stood Belinda under the shower and turned it on. Slowly the Duchess started to strip off her riding gear in front of Belinda. Like Belinda the Duchess was well endowed, but her ass was showing signs of her 50 something years, and childbirth had not been kind to her stomach muscles. However she was still in good shape and the

— Does the Duchess have a dick?

How do you guess someone's age from their ass? Is it like the rings on a tree trunk?

Is that a triple or quadruple negative? Either way, it makes no sense.

That's such a Dad thing to say. She used her Christmas smellies . . .

> **Language Alert—"My Lady"**
>
> The Duchess's insistence that Belinda call her "My Lady" could be interpreted as an homage to Milady de Winter from *The Three Musketeers*. Milady is Cardinal Richelieu's chief spy and assassin, amoral and dangerous. Does this suggest the Duchess is not to be trusted and may not be all she appears?

Does she think Belinda's tits are a soap dispenser?

riding clothes had made the most of her attributes. Belinda could not help but hope she would not be in worse shape when she reached the same age, albeit some twenty years away!

Now totally naked the Duchess started to wash Belinda and herself down with shampoo and smelly natural oils. Belinda whispered a word of thanks for this thoughtful act, even though the Duchess's hands were all over her vagina, ass and breasts. The Duchess immediately frowned and stepped out of the shower area to pick up her crop which was laid close to hand across the wash hand basin.

I'm guessing that word of thanks was "thanks."

'Address me as "My Lady" and nothing else!' and to emphasize this she flicked the crop onto the cheek of Belinda's right ass. The crop's impact made Belinda jump and left a nasty bright red mark on her skin. Belinda grimaced and replied quickly,

Has Belinda got two asses?

'Thank you My Lady.'

'That's better servant.' said the Duchess.

Oh God, it's getting a bit BDSM now.

The Duchess set the crop aside and continued to wash down Belinda, again applying plenty of hand squeezing to her tits. After five minutes of this the Duchess changed her tactics and concentrated on her vagina and clitoris. Belinda's nipples started to respond, she was after all, that type of girl and

Is that the most words
Belinda has used in a row
so far?

Has Belinda got varicose veins
she needs treating?

couldn't help it. However, the Duchess started to smile and said, 'That's very good servant.'

How long are they?

'Thank you My Lady.' replied Belinda.

With her nipples now (fully extended) and her vagina starting to become wet, the Duchess decided to dry down Belinda and move her to the bedroom. Belinda was told to lie down, open her legs wide and masturbate herself in front of the Duchess.

"Masturbate" is one of those words you think and hope your parents would never know or use.

'My Lady, please fuck me as you wish, I know I am your servant, so please use me for your pleasure.' said Belinda.

The Duchess smiled and said, 'Yes servant, I do believe you mean it, and I will test you soon, don't you worry!'

The Duchess seems a little creepy.

The Duchess left the room and Belinda looked around her. It was a classic motel bedroom, there was nothing to look at which would give her a clue as to where she was. She would just have to wait until the Duchess wanted to have sex with her and perhaps tell her where she was. The Duchess soon returned with two glasses of Gin and Tonic in her hands. She set them down, and started to massage Belinda's long legs. She stretched them out and quickly shackled her ankles to the bottom of the bed with a similar pair of handcuffs Tony had used on her that afternoon in the Maze. This

This doesn't sound sexy. It sounds like physiotherapy.

What? Like a tablecloth? They sound paper thin.

She's got napkin-thin breasts with bolts on the end, scratching her dry skin. How is this supposed to be erotic?

Cultural Context—Equestrian Erotica

There have been a number of romantic/erotic novels written over the years involving horses. Titles include *Tame Horses Wild Hearts*, *Unbridled Love: A Romance With Horse Sense*, *Texas Rein*, *One Wild Cowboy*, and, of course, *There's Something About Horses*. Why? Perhaps it's the kinky nature of the clothing and accoutrements (whips, long leather boots, etc.) of horse riding and show jumping. Or maybe it's the nature of the relationship between human and horse that reflects the dominant and submissive roles of BDSM.

Has she somehow read *Belinda Blinked*? Because I've never read about this before.

How strong is her tongue? Sounds like she's giving her a deep-tissue massage

time they were coloured yellow, Belinda wondered idly where they were purchasing them from... Toys Ur Us?

The Duchess started to massage Belinda's arms, it felt so good and she half expected them to be tied to the bedhead but this didn't happen and Belinda soon found out why. They finished their drinks, the Duchess who was also still totally naked, started to massage Belinda's body with her tongue. The Duchess's breasts draped over Belinda's body as she licked her from head to toe. Belinda found it strangely erotic, especially when the Duchess's nipples, now as hard as rivets scraped her soft skin. Belinda responded by rubbing her hand up and down the Duchess's vagina and eventually picked up enough courage to massage her clit.

Rave reviews. Sounds like a wild session.

After some very satisfactory moments according to the loud moans emanating from the Duchess, she stood up and left the room. Belinda started to wonder what she had done wrong, but the Duchess returned with her riding crop in hand. Belinda immediately thought that this was where it was going to get nasty. But being the servant of the Duchess didn't necessarily mean you were going to be whipped into a sexual frenzy. Instead the crop handle was to become a substitute penis. The Duchess smiled at Belinda and said 'Are you ready for this, servant?'

Belinda nodded her head slowly in disbelief, she had read about this type of sexual fantasy, but had never, ever experienced it.

Understatement of the century. ——

Only the best for Belinda. ——————

This book feels like an eternity. ——————

Wasn't that about an hour ago? ——————

Some sales job this was turning out to be! The Duchess wasted no more time and pressed the crop handle into Belinda's vagina. Belinda jumped as she hadn't had really enough foreplay to make her wet enough to receive this size of object. However she grinned and said,

'Thanks My Lady.' She also wickedly thought, 'I must send Jim Stirling one of these.' *Great comedy timing from Belinda. Poor Jim!*

Belinda started to grind onto the leather crop handle, in actual real life experiences the handle was smaller than a lot of the cocks she had encountered. The Duchess held it in position and let Belinda enjoy the experience while she sucked her breasts and ate her nipples. The Duchess became more vigorous with the leather crop and Belinda became very wet, orgasming at least three times in quick succession. After some ten minutes the crop was withdrawn and the Duchess licked it all over. *The Duchess thinks she's at a buffet.*

Satisfied, she then walked over to the wardrobe and brought out a strap on penis again made of finest leather. She put it on and entered Belinda in a single thrust. This time Belinda knew she was in for a real hammering and took what felt like an eternity of heavy thrusting, it was truly the best ride she had experienced since the Dutchman Peter Rouse. The Duchess then unlocked Belinda's ankles from their plastic shackles and expertly flipped her onto her front. She started to massage Belinda's back and buttocks.

All four of them??

What's with all the health
and safety checks? It's not
a roller coaster. ————————

And not a second more! ———————

Because manners are still important
when you're pounding someone with a
strap-on. ———————

Like a pair of curtains? ———————

Because there's nothing sexier
than a friction burn. ———————

She's in and out like a fiddler's elbow! ———————

After a fairly short time the Duchess said to Belinda, 'OK servant it's your turn'. Belinda couldn't believe what she was hearing and watched warily whilst the Duchess removed the straps and put the penis onto Belinda. The Duchess made sure everything was tight and in the right place and slapped Belinda's ass as a gesture of good to go. *Like a horse?*

There's a phrase I didn't think I'd read.

Belinda walked around the bedroom with her monster prick out in front of her. She could hardly believe it and happily got to work on the Duchess, first in a standing position, giving it as hard as she had had it all that day. After about seven minutes of pounding the Duchess's vagina and cervix, Belinda asked her to get onto her knees, still remembering to call her 'My Lady'.

'Now hold your tits apart using your nipples My Lady'. Belinda then slid the leather penis up and down between the Duchess's breasts making sure there was a lot of friction taking place. After about five minutes of this technique the Duchess's skin became red and chaffed. 'True justice for keeping me in those plastic handcuffs.' thought Belinda.

And cervix? Vagina's fine—no need to go any deeper.

Bit harsh! Poor Duchess.

In fairness Belinda thought the old bird was not doing too badly, but she didn't let up on the pressure. She had always felt that the British aristocracy needed pain to make any sexual experience worthwhile. She also knew if she didn't give her mistress what she wanted, she would end up back in the cuffs tied to the bed. Belinda entered her vagina again and took her for another five minutes. The Duchess groaned and held her long legs wide for more.

Who's timing this? Someone got a stopwatch?

Is the Duchess's vagina
a revolving door? ——————————

Like crumpled bits of paper. ——————————

Why's everyone using breasts as handles?

That's not entirely unusual. Belinda arrives
most places totally naked. ——————

Take cover—she's gonna blow!

'OK' thought Belinda, 'it's time for a couple of (volcanic orgasms) and she entered her mistress's vagina again. The dildo penetrated her cervix whilst stimulating her clitoris and the Duchess quickly orgasmed for her first time.

Belinda kept up the stimulation and soon the Duchess had orgasmed four times. She stammered 'Thank you servant, that was utterly fantastic.' Belinda came out of her and looked at the Duchess's face, she looked totally shattered, her make up was ruined and her immaculate hair was all over the place. Belinda then held her tits hard in her hands and pulled her into an upright position. The Duchess flopped back onto the bed, (No stamina.) thought Belinda. Then to Belinda's surprise her mistress immediately fell asleep. Belinda had obviously worn her out and suddenly thought what do I do now? She was free to leave, or was she?

I know how she feels.

Give the woman a break—she's in her fifties!

Has she got narcolepsy?

Belinda thought for a few moments and an idea entered her head. She took the discarded yellow handcuffs and put them on the Duchess's ankles. The Duchess didn't stir throughout this procedure and was now sleeping very deeply.

Something's actually happening. Is this going to become a story?

'Perfect.' thought Belinda, 'she should stay this way for at least four or five hours which will take me past my twelve hour servant contract'.

The second part of Belinda's plan was simple. As she had arrived at the chalet totally naked she had no clothing and needed something to get

No surprise there. She very
rarely wears underwear.

Belinda, give it a rest for two
seconds. She's sex mad!

You don't need to accessorize!
Just get dressed!

The Duchess is totally conked out.

Belinda's sexy weekend in a caravan has to
be a spin-off book, surely?

back to the Horse and Jockey for her late evening appointment with Peter Rouse. Calmly Belinda went to the wet room and picked up the Duchess's discarded riding clothes and boots. They would fit her just fine and she didn't need to wear the underwear. She quickly pulled on the jodhpurs and riding boots. Standing up she looked at herself in the large mirror… 'Not bad' she thought, 'Indeed they look very sexy' the black boots suited her colouring and the elasticated jodhpurs took the shape of her perfect ass extremely well. She pulled on the white blouse and attached the black cravat around the collar. Lastly she put on the red riding jacket, it indeed was a beauty and must have cost a small fortune. A last look in the mirror told Belinda what she already instinctively knew… she looked a million dollars.

She looks like a discount from a bargain bin at best.

She checked on the now snoring Duchess, grabbed the back riding cap and crop, switched off the lights and left the chalet. As she had hoped the Duchess had left the keys in the ignition. Belinda had no need for the horsebox so she unhooked it and mentally thanked one of her past male flings for teaching her how to caravan. She jumped into the driving seat, started up the engine, put on the headlights and headed for the main road. All she needed now was a signpost to the local town where she could orientate herself, find the Horse and Jockey and keep her appointment with Peter.

CHARACTER PROFILE: The Duchess

It is universally acknowledged that the British aristocracy are generally eccentric and the Duchess is no exception. This is immediately brought to the reader's attention through her flamboyant fashion sense. When we meet her she is wearing a white linen trouser suit and a panama hat, much like the man from the famous Del Monte adverts of the 1980s. Not much later she changes into full horse-riding gear, hinting at her keen interest in all things equestrian.

A woman in her fifties (or an "old bird" as Flintstone unflatteringly describes her), the Duchess is also a mother, although it is not revealed how many children she has. She is a mysterious presence at the tombola and her motives behind bidding for Belinda are unclear. However, what does quickly become clear is that the Duchess is a kinky lover, favoring toys and whips in her sexual encounters and insisting Belinda call her "My Lady."

She is also a terrible driver, although this could have something to do with the fact she has had a gin and tonic (her tipple of choice) before getting behind the wheel of her four-by-four.

• **Physical Attribute:** Two-ply tits

• **Dominant Character Trait:** Regal bisexual

• **Unusual Skill:** Adept with a dildo

• **Fun Fact:** Enjoys shagging, sobbing, and sleeping

🔓 KEY THEME: Dildos

The earliest dildos are believed to date back to Upper Paleolithic times, nearly 30,000 years ago. Early dildos were made of stone, tar, wood, and other firm materials that could be shaped as penises. Ancient Greeks even used a dildo made of bread.

Dildos were referenced in literature as early as the 1590s, when English playwright Thomas Nashe wrote a poem known as "The Merrie Ballad of Nashe, His Dildo." Shakespeare also makes reference to them in Act IV, Scene IV of *The Winter's Tale*.

Modern dildos are made from many different materials, including glass, chrome-plated steel (popular in the BDSM scene), and silicone rubber. Silicone rubber dildos are the most inexpensive, making them the perfect choice for a first-time user.

The possession and sale of dildos is illegal in some jurisdictions, including India. Interestingly, the American state of Alabama prohibits the sale of sex toys to this day. Furthermore, in Japan, many dildos are created to resemble animals or cartoon characters, so that they may be sold as toys, thus avoiding obscenity laws.

 **ACTIVITY**

Find a local caravan and practice hooking it to a car using the following instructions:

1. Ensure the caravan hand brake is on.

2. Use the jockey wheel to raise the caravan hitch height until it is above the car-tow ball.

3. Reverse the car, bringing the tow ball underneath the caravan hitch. Put the car's handbrake on.

4. Raise the hitch lever and lower the hitch on to the tow ball by winding up the jockey wheel.

5. Keep winding the jockey wheel up until the hitch fits over the tow ball, and the hitch-safety mechanism pops out, showing green, or in older types until the handle clicks back into place.

6. To check you have locked on properly, wind down the jockey wheel until the rear of the car starts to lift.

AUTHOR'S NOTE

Where does the equestrian influence in your writing come from?

I actually grew up in the countryside, and while horses weren't a part of my everyday life, they were around. Anyone who was fairly well off would own a horse and take it out fox hunting or racing at the annual tombola. The horse to me represents money, affluence, and an aristocratic bearing. They're lovely animals and are the ideal way for Belinda to develop her social network, which will bring in even huger bonuses. There is also an awful lot of British life and fashion revolving around the horse and this gives me the opportunity to develop her friends, such as the Duchess, in various plot directions.

Rocky x

Reading group discussion points

- Compare and contrast the sexual approaches of Belinda and the Duchess. What does it say about their attitudes to life?

- The Duchess has flamboyant fashion sense. List celebrities who dress flamboyantly and discuss what this reflects about their personality.

- Are you pro- or anti-aristocracy? Debate the reasons for your stance.

- Reflect on the plot of *Belinda Blinked 1* at this stage. What has/hasn't happened? Where do you expect the story to go? Do you care?

How vague. It's your novel, give him an age!

It's 8 p.m. What restaurant stops serving at 8:20?! That's prime time.

CHAPTER 10

The Horse and Jockey;

Of course they are. Being "true to their word" is their only function.

The signposts were true to their word and Belinda soon found her way to the Horse and Jockey. She maneuvered the large car into one of the parking spaces, cut the engine and found her way to reception. It was now 8pm and she asked the youngish man on duty if dinner was still serving.

Ten points to Belinda.

'There's still twenty more minutes left for orders madam, and might I add how extremely attractive you are looking this evening'. Belinda grinned and wondered if he had recognized the clothes or was just fishing for a bit of sex later on that night, whatever, she didn't want to disappoint so she replied,

Belinda is so arrogant—she construes even a kindly word as a sexual advance.

'Why thank you, how very gentlemanly of you to say so, especially as I'm dining alone!'

He smiled in return and nodded slowly as if confirming he might be available that evening.

I feel like I'm living on the edge. This time frame is SO tight. Don't make a reservation, JUST SIT DOWN. T-minus seventeen minutes till kitchen closes.

The stolen clothes of an old-aged pensioner? Yeah, it'll be on the catwalks of Milan in no time.

Finally some urgency. T-minus nine minutes.

Wine's the bar's jurisdiction!!!! Order a fucking starter!!! T-minus two minutes.

There are certain things a father should never show his child. Not that I'm exactly in a position to judge.

She doesn't have time to "eat at her leisure." Unless her food's been blended and served intravenously, that is.

'Please book me in for dinner, I'll be down in ten minutes.'

'Certainly Madam.'

She better be bloody quick.
T-minus thirteen minutes.

Belinda asked for her key and went immediately to her room, she quickly spruced herself up and viewed the mirror. Yes she agreed, I do look extremely attractive in a very raw sexy way in this riding gear. I think this is a must new style for me, hopefully Peter Rouse will feel the same.

Pride before a fall,
Belinda.

However there was no time to lose, she was famished, she hadn't eaten since that very quick lunchtime BBQ and she needed strength for the rest of what was going to be a very active evening. She ran down to the dining room, got shown her table and immediately ordered a bottle of Chardonnay, Chilean of course. Belinda prided herself on knowing her wines, her father after all was a sales manager for one of the big wine cellars in central London and he had spent many evenings training her in one of the best sales techniques for getting clients to buy without remorse. Drinking very good wine… and lots of it!

T-minus
four minutes.

I knew Dad
would worm
his favorite
tipple in here
somewhere,
the old soak.

Belinda dined at her leisure and for the first time that day she felt she wasn't under pressure, though her strange clothing didn't fit all that well and made her feel quite hot. She couldn't wait to start removing some of it she thought wickedly. Her meal finished Belinda took the rest of her wine to her room in an ice bucket where she sipped it slowly.

It's possible the Duchess didn't anticipate
you robbing her blind so didn't take the
time to have it tailored for you, Belinda.

She's been drinking white wine alone for two hours and forty minutes. I'm no mathematician but that equals a hot mess.

Yes, because she's the only one there.

Yeah, that would be a mood killer. "Straight after I had sex with you I went to the Duchess's house and she stuck a riding crop up me."

And a couple of other things: "I've stolen her car and left her unconscious at her motel. But how's your day been?"

Language Alert

To "pique your interest" is a common phrase in the English-speaking world. Here Flintstone has cleverly flipped the expression to reference the "tweaking" of "nipple tips" [sic] and other such sexual activities depicted in the novel.

Maybe just one glass of water?

It was now 11.00pm and it was time for Peter to make an appearance.
Belinda went down to the lobby where she ordered another bottle of
Chardonnay, popped it into the replenished ice bucket and waited for
Peter. Spot on at 11.30 he walked through the lobby door and saw Belinda
immediately. He opened his hands and kissed her on the cheek, both
sides…not unusual for a sophisticated European.

I think people would reserve that phrase for their mum's best friend's daughter's husband. Not someone who did them a topknot using their sperm.

'Would you like a drink Mr. Rouse?

'Oh please keep calling me Peter, after all we are very much acquainted after
this afternoons events. Have I told you, you have a wonderful body my dear,
and much, much better without the mud!'

At. What?

They both laughed and Peter said,

'I do like your current outfit Belinda…very much in tune with this hotel.'

Their small talk's run dry already.

Belinda gently blushed, she couldn't tell him how she had acquired the
clothing, and she really did enjoy wearing it.

'I do like wearing adventurous garments Peter and I hoped these would
tweak your interest!'

'Top marks! Is that what they say in the show jumping circles?' *No.*

What, in the lobby? Literally get a room.

So he put his order in BEFORE he put his "order" in? Awkward.

Belinda replied quickly,

'I'm more of a fox chasing type of person myself!'   *Alert me when that begins.*

'Ha ha ha… very good Belinda, I do enjoy your style of humour.. now let's have some of that delicious wine.'   *And a black coffee for the lady.*

Belinda poured Peter a glass and leant back on the leather settee. Peter sat beside her and gently fondled her left thigh. Belinda decided to get round to business quickly, before she lost her tentative female advantage.

The classic TFA???!!! Whatever that is.

'Peter, could we position some of our pots and pans range in your supermarkets?'   *Oh, for the first time she actually meant business. Finally.*

'Absolutely', Peter replied, 'In fact this afternoon we've just ordered 3000 units of your Oxy Brillo range to get you started, and my purchasing team are looking at other products of yours which will fit into our present range of kitchen utensils.

'Wow!' Belinda gasped and opened her legs slightly.

Peter quickly took advantage and moved his hand higher up her thigh. Belinda undid her cravat and slowly unbuttoned the top four of her shirt buttons. Her delicious cleavage was now on view. Peter quickly moved his

That would be the entire blouse then.

Is it like a game of Twister? "Left hand to upper thigh. Right hand to left breast."

While cradling a boob is no time to criticize your price point.

Belinda has scheduled visits to Brussels, Texas, and now Amsterdam, all in the next three weeks. She's just thinking of the air miles.

other hand to fondle her left breast and rubbed the nipple showing through
the white linen.

The opposite of their sales director.

'No problem Belinda, after all your company's products are top class if a
little expensive and I'm sure we can overcome that little problem between
us.'

You think you've got a relationship and then they invoice you.

'Yes!' Belinda gasped, her senses working overtime between Peter's
massaging her very upper thigh and breast.

Vagina?

'I have access to some marketing incentives which will help.'

Seriously. Just shut up.

'Shhh, Belinda, just relax,' said Peter, 'we can discuss this all at the office
next week in Amsterdam when you come to visit me.'

'Am I?' replied Belinda, 'Oh yes of course, I really can't wait!'

'Well let's make it Thursday, OK?'

*Her diary's pretty full actually,
Peter. Get in the queue.*

'Yes, yes, I'll be there.'

'But now,' said Peter, 'let's get down to some real business.'

It should read: "He slowly walked her out of the lobby and up to her bedroom."

Like a couple of rugby balls.

Drink! Why not. Belinda is.

Her mind thought? SHE thought.

Cultural Context

The turn of the millennium and democratization of media through smartphones and the Internet led to a surge in the "celebrity sex tape" culture. With this plot twist Belinda is joining the esteemed company of Kim Kardashian, Paris Hilton, and Pamela Anderson.

Dressing and undressing her simultaneously. That's like taking down her trousers while tying her shoes.

He slowly unbuttoned the remaining buttons on Belinda's shirt and let her full oval breasts fall out. In one fluid movement he tucked her shirt into the back of her jodhpurs and started kissing her. Belinda groaned, she could never resist the soft male touch of a mouth on her nipples, and Peter was exquisite in his sensuality.

Belinda would be GOLD in the Big Brother house.

Above his head in the corner of the lobby Belinda noticed a red light blinking… it was a security camera, no doubt recording what was going on. Her mind thought of the young man behind the desk when she checked in… yes that was it, he was building his profile of her for his personal use. A wicked thought entered her mind, she would give him a session to record, and Peter Rouse a very good time into the bargain.

-ish

No, it's to protect the patrons against thieves. I'm looking at you, Miss Blumenthal.

143

The Horse & Jockey ££ ★☆☆☆

This converted outhouse situated in the picturesque rolling hills of Oxfordshire is a stone's throw from the ancestral family home of the Godwin dynasty.

Old-fashioned and in need of renovation, rooms are fully equipped with sumptuous beds, en-suites and 24-hour room service.

Top tip: don't be caught out by the unorthodox dinner serving times. Also, patrons are advised to keep an eye on their belongings as thieves frequent the establishment, though there is a higher than average security presence.

KEY THEME: Hospitality and Catering

British culture has long been synonymous with terrible food, and this was never more pertinent than with public houses. Traditionally pubs were drinking establishments and if they served meals at all they were simple cold dishes, such as cockles, a ploughman's lunch, or pickled eggs. The invention of gastropubs in the 1990s revived the British pub scene and countless rural eateries have thrived in the twenty-first century. These restaurants tend to specialize in old English favorites, such as fish and chips, steak and ale pie, and turkey sandwiches.

AUTHOR'S NOTE

Why is wine, specifically Chilean Chardonnay, Belinda's drink of choice?

Personally I love wine and in a previous life have even been a sommelier. That's why wine is used to lubricate Belinda's social intercourse with her clients. It's an important facet of modern-day life and one I wholeheartedly prescribe to. My favorite is Chardonnay, especially heavily oaked, which is not so much in vogue today. With Belinda I want to revive it and get it away from the tarty footballer image it sort of has.

I adore English B & Bs. I actually eschew the corporate hotel scene in place of bed-and-breakfasts/small hotels. I remember once subscribing to a great little book called *Staying off the Beaten Track*; it was simply splendid.

Rocky x

⛰ KEY SETTING: The Horse and Jockey Pub

Unlike Thomas Hardy, Flintstone rarely describes locations for their own sake. The description of the interview room in Chapter 1, for example, concentrates solely on the "elegant wooden coat racks." However, the reader is afforded one notable exception to this trend when, as Dickensian London or *Sex and the City*'s New York, the Horse and Jockey pub becomes a character in its own right.

In 2015 Flintstone cited Hampstead public house the Spaniards Inn as an influence for the setting of Belinda and Peter's late-night liaison. This is notable given the literary history of the north London watering hole; the pub is mentioned in Dickens's *The Pickwick Papers*, Bram Stoker's *Dracula*, and legend states that John Keats wrote his ballad "Ode to a Nightingale" in the beer garden.

With *Belinda Blinked 1*, the Spaniards Inn has inspired another legendary author to create a truly iconic setting.

Reading group discussion points

- In pairs, discuss whether Belinda and Peter's relationship is healthy for business.

- Hollywood star Elijah Wood has actively lobbied for the role of the Youngish Man in the big-screen adaptation of *Belinda Blinked 1*. Who would you cast as Belinda?

- A hotel lobby is the setting for a sexual tryst this chapter. Have you ever been intimate in a public place?

- Flintstone presents two different sides to Belinda in Chapter 10. How do you view Belinda at this stage of the novel?

- Explore the theme of intimacy through the different perspectives held by Belinda and Peter.

Language Alert

The first recorded use of "randy" with the meaning "lewd, lustful" was in 1847. *First and last time anyone's ever used it.*

Can anyone be passionate and just throw stuff on the floor? _____
We don't need a full laundry service.

Have we all forgotten about the camera?? ——————

CHAPTER 11

Sunday Night 11.55pm;

Belinda groaned more loudly,

'Peter, that's so good, would you mind removing my riding jacket and shirt?'

Most proper novels have spelling mistakes, right?

Peter was already feeling randy and he promptly striped Belinda of her upper garments. He folded them neatly, and placed the already discarded cravat on top of them on a nearby table. The lobby was very quiet, Sunday night at just about midnight meant the clients had all retired to bed, he felt he had a free rein to do what he needed to do. *It's not a necessity.*

I suppose Belinda's breasts go through similar toils to an Olympian's muscles. They should probably have an ice bath.

'Massage me.' continued Belinda 'My tits so need a good massage.' Peter acquiesced and concentrated his hands on her upper body. It was a firm body with lots of good muscle and superb rock hard nipples, he thought to himself, she'll need these nipples if she's going to make the sales she wants.

As opposed to the jobs where you don't need nipples?

He'll chip a crown in a minute!

I beg your pardon??????????

Language Alert

In a way that perhaps seems uncharacteristic, Belinda is asserting herself in this chapter—her language is strong and direct. By using declaratives, e.g., "strip me," "massage me," "take off the riding boots," Flintstone is reestablishing Belinda's power within the romantic duo.

Imagine checking in late and seeing THAT.

Literally Pandora's box.

Belinda's vagina is like Home Alone 2—everyone has seen it.

Treat it like a newly sown lawn. Always keep it irrigated.

EVEN more loudly?
It must be deafening!

Belinda groaned more loudly and watched the movement of the camera and its blinking red light out of the corner of her eye.

'Peter, strip me, I so need to feel your hand on my clitoris, handle my cervix hard.' Again Peter acquiesced and gently pulled down the jodhpurs to the top of Belinda's black leather riding boots.

'No,' Belinda gasped, 'everything… take off the riding boots.' Peter took his hands off her jodhpurs and pulled first at her left boot and then her right boot. With both successfully removed it only took a second to pull the jodhpurs off Belinda's body.

Like a sexy hokey pokey.

At last he had her completely naked lying in front of him on the hotel lobby leather sofa. Belinda slowly moved her legs apart showing him her seductive vagina and all the mysteries he was about to again discover.

Like the hands on a Swiss watch.

'Pass me my glass of Chardonnay.' Belinda drank it all in one go and calmly poured the remaining few drops over her vagina. She rubbed the golden liquid into her soft tanned flesh and beckoned Peter to taste it. Behind his head Belinda observed the camera recording the event.

Why wouldn't she be calm?

Peter Rouse was no mean artist when it came to sexual activity, but never before had he been so completely entranced by such a beautiful female. He had no doubt in his own mind that he had come here to seduce her but this

What even is that?

So he thought, we really should go to the room, but in the meantime . . . cunnilingus, Belinda?!

How do we break it to Peter? It's not her first orgasm of the night.

He's finally run out of synonyms, so he's started making them up.

Realized?! What is it? Adam and Eve?

one was different, could he have met his equal in his sexual symbolic world?

He shook his head, there was no way this girl was not his equal, she was better than all the others, he had to stick to his plan and attempt to make himself dominant over her. But he couldn't do it in a public hotel lobby, he needed a private room away from prying people and no doubt hidden security cameras.

Finally we can agree on something.

They're not prying; they're just trying to check in.

After five or six minutes of massaging Belinda's clitoris with his tongue he tasted the first orgasm Belinda had that night. It was so sweet, yet bitter. As an aphrodisiac he needed nothing else… except complete privacy. Belinda was now moaning consistently and Peter, still fully clothed, continued to massage her vagina and breast nipples. Each in their turn… and making sure to never let the sexual pressure he had now so carefully built decline.

At last he had had enough.

That's weird. I had by line 3, Chapter 1.

Isn't that a flavor of Sweet Tarts!? Oh, wait, no, that's Good & Plenty. False alarm.

'Belinda, I want you, I want all your body with my body and we need to retire to your room.'

Are these wedding vows?

'Peter, I thought you'd never ask.' replied Belinda winking at the silent camera.

Some things you can just take for granted.

They both slowly stood up and realized Belinda was completely naked and Peter was completely dressed.

What would they look like exactly?

Nice repetition of "completely" to absolutely no effect.

'We must look completely stupid.' Peter exclaimed.

Another corker from Peter.

Yeah, for God's sake don't let anyone see your shoulders; leave the vagina out on show.

Belinda burst out laughing and said, 'Pass me my riding jacket and boots'. She put on the jacket which neatly covered up her breasts and then pulled on both leather riding boots which hid nothing except her lower legs and toes. *So, boots then.*

'Very daring!' said Peter with a laugh and collected the unfinished wine in its ice bucket.

Walking past the reception area, Peter asked Belinda if she would like a nightcap as well as another bottle of wine. They both decided on brandy and the youngish man behind reception poured the golden liquid into two impeccable glasses. He said he would bring up the wine to Belinda's room as soon as he located some more ice. Peter now carrying both glasses of the swirling golden brown liquid followed Belinda's seductively swaying ass up the main staircase to her room.

Has he been there the whole time??

Anyone else picturing a camel?

Once inside, Belinda immediately removed her red jacket and asked Peter to do the honours with her riding boots.

'Have a sip first my dear, it's too good to delay any longer.' Belinda sat down on the edge of the bed and sipped her brandy.

Can it be aroused separately from him?———

Cultural Context

There are key differences between a massage for sports injuries and those during sexual play. Namely the former should not initiate sexual arousal and the latter would not necessarily improve a groin strain; in fact, it could severely exacerbate it.

Language Alert

The pubic bone is a constituent part of the pelvis. It is covered by a fat layer, which is then covered by the rounded mass of fatty tissue known as the mons pubis. *sexy.*

She just asked you to take them off, but whatever.

'Besides, I'd like to fuck you with your boots on... they're extremely sexual in their own way you know!'

Belinda murmured 'If only you knew their origins.' and lay back on the bed anticipating Peter's desire.

Is everything Velcro?

He's going to kill her! That's so far north!

It only took Peter Rouse twenty five seconds to remove his clothes and position himself beside Belinda on the bed, he grabbed her cervix, his penis was already well aroused and Belinda knew it would only take a little bit of extra encouragement to make it rock solid. She started to massage his chest, concentrating on his nipples. She then dipped her right forefinger into her brandy glass and rubbed it onto his upper body making a delicate figure of eight in a clockwise motion over his stomach. Peter relaxed, lay on his back and let Belinda's tongue follow the pattern of the brandy.

More symbols!

His cock shuddered and Belinda lifted herself onto it. Slowly, slowly she went down on his hard penis and when she felt it had fully entered her she started to grind her pubic bone against his. Peter started to groan in time to her motion, his voice became more intense as Belinda increased the friction between their two bodies. Within a minute he orgasmed and white semen came trickling out of Belinda's vagina.

Disappointing.

Just in case we thought it was that radioactive green stuff from Ghostbusters.

Has he fallen asleep still inside her?? ————

What are you suggesting, Peter? ————

That's completely Belinda's mantra. ————

Belinda immediately caught the escaping liquid with her forefinger and once again traced the figure of eight pattern onto Peter's abdomen. He groaned more deeply and cried out as if in torment,

'More, more, more... Belinda!

Yes, exactly.

Sshhh, my darling Peter, you will get as much as you need, trust me!

Belinda continued the deep sexual movement until Peter again orgasmed, this time very deeply. Within seconds he had fallen unconscious, deeply asleep and Belinda withdrew her vagina knowing she had hit the target.

Was that bittersweet taste chloroform?

It took Peter Rouse one complete hour to wake up and when he did he felt as if he had shed twenty years of his life. He felt so energetic, so composed, so fulfilled. He looked around the hotel bedroom until he saw the naked Belinda, sitting on a casual chair watching him wake up

He's thinking, SHIIIIIIT.

'Belinda, Belinda,' he stammered, 'that was stupendous, I feel so very good, so very alive, what did you do to me?'

''Peter, we just had good old fashioned sex... it was what we both wanted, and when you get what you want, you feel great!'

I did not see that coming; is this ... a twist in the plot?!

Talking Point

Belinda and Peter seem to have found a prime love match, when he drops the bombshell about his marital status. The doomed relationship is a theme visited over and over in great works of literature. Tragic couples range from Vronsky and Anna in *Anna Karenina* by Leo Tolstoy to Gatsby and Daisy in *The Great Gatsby* by F. Scott Fitzgerald. But perhaps none are as ill suited as Rouse and Blumenthal.

How much faster could he have been? Twenty-five seconds to get his clothes off, and one minute to get his rocks off!

Peter nodded slowly, as if realizing he had missed something important, but couldn't just quite remember what it was.

'Ok, but thank you, very, very much.'

'Peter, it's all my pleasure and thank you for your business order.'

'Belinda, it's nothing, but could you excuse me, I do need to get back to my wife, we both didn't expect me to be out for so long.'

Belinda smiled and said, 'Peter that's no problem, I'll see you Thursday afternoon in your Amsterdam offices.'

Doesn't give a shit.

'That's a date.' He replied, 'I'm so looking forward to it, but you must experience Amsterdam at night and we'll get you back to London on the <u>late afternoon Friday flight.</u>' —— *Just a bit of admin before the chapter is through.*

'I'll make the arrangements and bring some evening wear.'

'Not too much, Belinda, not too much.' said Peter as he let himself out of the room.

I don't think Belinda bringing too many clothes is ever a concern.

Female Reproductive System

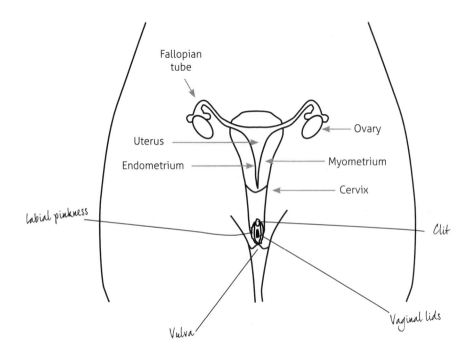

Fallopian tube

Uterus

Endometrium

Ovary

Myometrium

Cervix

Labial pinkness

Clit

Vulva

Vaginal lids

⊘ CULTURAL CONTEXT
Cervix (see diagram)

The cervix is the lower part of the uterus, which joins to the top of the vagina. The opening of the cervix allows blood to flow from the vagina during menstruation. In pregnant women it is closed to help keep the fetus in the uterus until the time of birth. Around half the cervix is visible with suitable medical apparatus; the rest lies above the vagina, far from view. Its structural integrity should not be compromised by grabbing, jabbing, or stabbing.

The cervix has been documented anatomically since at least the time of Hippocrates, over two millennia ago. So it is not clear why Flintstone has no idea where it is or what function it performs.

⊙ KEY THEME: Foreplay

Peter Rouse is fully aware of the power of foreplay, using the time at the beginning of each sexual encounter to build arousal and excitement for both himself and Belinda. Whether this be through prodding, probing, or groping, his approach is clear: in sex, as in business, never a second should be wasted. Not all of these moments of sexual prep are physical—some can also be psychological, and he uses his mental connection with Belinda to great effect.

AUTHOR'S NOTE

How do you create a scene that is passionate?

I take it as a compliment that people think that this chapter is quite hot and heavy. I felt it was important to revisit and to emphasize the sexual nature of this erotic novella. Creating a great sex scene is all about the words; without the right words, such as "cervix" and "vulva," a good erotic writer would be nowhere. It's also important to have the characters properly dressed and to undress them without skipping too many of the actions this involves. If you want it racy, undress them faster; if you want it more romantic, then undress them slower. It's as simple as that!

ACTIVITY

Print out a picture of the female reproductive system and stick it to the wall. From a separate piece of paper cut out an image of the cervix, attaching a drawing pin to it. Blindfold a member of the gathering, spin them thrice, and see if they can pin the cervix on the vagina.

Reading group discussion points

- How do the styles of sexual play represent the characters' respective personalities?

- Who in the book group do you think is "no mean artist"?

- How long is too fast to remove all your clothes?

- Who is in control in this chapter?

- How do you think Belinda felt when Peter mentioned his wife?

Cultural Context

In trying to estimate the Youngish Man's age, it is helpful to refer to the Dating Equation. This rule defines that it is acceptable to be romantically connected to someone half your age plus seven and no lower. As Belinda is twenty-nine, using this formula the Youngish Man could be no younger than twenty-one.

Cultural Context

Flintstone revealed in an interview that another favorite late-night snack is beef on white sliced bread with lashings of English mustard.

CHAPTER 12

The Night Receptionist;

Belinda put on her riding jacket, jodhpurs and leather boots, sat down in the corner chair and slowly sipped the rest of her unfinished brandy. Sure enough five minutes later there was a knock on her door.

Isn't it 2 a.m.? It's probably time for bed, Belinda.

'Room service, Madam.' — *Pretty sure what she's about to be served isn't on the menu.*

'Come in please.'

Will we ever know his name??

The youngish man on reception entered the room with a trolley on which sat the ice bucket with a full bottle of Chilean Chardonnay. Beside it sat two rounds of what looked like turkey sandwiches, one of Belinda's many favourite late night snacks

Dad does love a bit of turkey. On the twenty-fifth of every month, we have a full Christmas dinner.

'My sincere apologies for the lateness of the hour, but the ice machine started to play up Madam.'

Talking Point

Thirty seconds is a long time in conversation. Try having a discussion in which your partner can't reply for thirty seconds. How does this affect the flow of the chat?

Language Alert—"Similar Vigour"

In phonaesthetics "similar vigour" is an example of a phrase that is beautiful purely in terms of its sound without regard for meaning. J. R. R. Tolkien once cited "cellar door" as the most beautiful combination of words in the English language.

This is the FIFTH person Belinda has shagged TODAY.

'I'm sure it did young man, don't apologise, your timing is appropriate, and I hope it's not the first time tonight it will be so!' It took about thirty seconds *THIRTY seconds?!* for the receptionist to understand Belinda's remark and he burst into a wide grin.

'I understand Madam, thank you.' With that he shut the door, walked over to Belinda and kissed her on the lips.

Like she's holding a baby?

Belinda took his head in her left hand and returned the kiss with a similar vigour. He put his hands around her waist and pulled her body into his. She could feel his cock throbbing with excitement as they drew closer, but she did feel a tad hungry after her couple of hours with Peter. Slowly she let him go and said,

Is it wriggling around like a cat in a bag?

'It would be a pity to waste such a good wine and these wonderful sandwiches… have you eaten tonight?'

'In actual fact I haven't.' he replied, 'I tend to satisfy my sexual appetite first and then eat.'

She should be careful—sex is like swimming. You have to wait for two hours after food.

'Well in that case I think we'll break the rules just a little, here and now.' Belinda reached over and took a sandwich, at the same time she unbuttoned the only single button on her riding jacket. Her breasts once again fell out

169

A glass of wine and a turkey sandwich in the worst hotel in England—the Youngish Man has such small dreams.

She only asked for the trousers.

Where else would they go?

and stayed on show whilst she finished the sandwich. The youngish man took one as well and poured them both a glass of wine.

He sat on the edge of the bed and announced,

Was it a footlong?

'You can't beat the high life!' Belinda laughed and toasted him with her half empty glass. One sandwich was enough for Belinda and she removed her riding jacket. She watched the instantaneous response in the youngish man's trousers and asked him to remove them. He obliged, but also took off his shirt, pants, shoes and socks. Now standing naked before her, she called him over. Belinda took his erect penis and gently rubbed cold chardonnay onto it. In fairness to the youngish man he didn't flinch and Belinda put his cock between her breasts. Using her two hands she squeezed both breasts together tightly and started to masturbate his penis.

BOING

She's obsessed with using alcohol as lube.

Same amount of time it takes him to get a joke.

It only took half a minute for him to start groaning. His hands fondled her long black hair bringing it up to the top of her head and letting it fall time after time. However to Belinda's surprise he didn't ejaculate and she guessed she'd have to work a bit harder to get that result.

Give the guy a chance!

Good thing she had that turkey sandwich for energy.

'Would you mind removing my riding boots… it enables me to pull down my jodhpurs you see.' He nodded understanding immediately and helped pull them off Belinda's legs and feet. By now Belinda had lost count of the

Oh, THAT he gets straight away.

Weathered, worn, and tatty—I suppose she is getting like a pair of old boots.

It's grown so large it's now been described as a region rather than an area. Belinda's vagina has its own postcode.

His tongue is Sputnik and Belinda's vagina is the Final Frontier.

— She's not the only one.

times she had pulled on or pulled off these riding boots in the past ten hours, but she thought they were getting more supple each time. Perhaps like her own body she mused.

'Ravish me!' she commanded the youngish man, and he immediately removed her jodhpurs. Now naked he followed the black line of pubic hair to Belinda's vaginal region. He got down on his knees, pushed her legs apart and gently started probing her clitoris with his tongue. Belinda once again that evening groaned softly at the foreign invasion of her pubic area. But this time it was different she thought, this unexpected pleasure was for her and her only… a perfect way to end a busy working day. No business deals, no reputations to be lost or offended, just a plain simple fucking session.

What a weird metaphor. Sounds like a game of Risk.

Is that Dad's version of a fairy tale "happily ever after"?

CHARACTER PROFILE: The Youngish Man

The Youngish Man is employed at the Horse and Jockey Hotel in Windsor. He appears to work every available shift on the reception desk, although he is best known for his work as the night receptionist. We are left to speculate about his age and Flintstone's definition of "youngish," prompting readers to guess at anything between eighteen and fifty-seven years old.

His only story arc is the turbulent time he has trying to repair the hotel's only ice machine. He manages to fix the problem but the source of the issue is never revealed. The Youngish Man is the only person Belinda sleeps with that day whom she has nothing to gain from. He offers respite from a seemingly endless day with potential business clients. It is, as Flintstone describes, "just a plain simple fucking session" and perhaps an attempt to fill the book's word count.

- **Physical Attribute:** Looks between 18 and 57

- **Dominant Character Trait:** A desire to serve

- **Unusual Skill:** Fixing mechanical equipment

- **Fun Fact:** His name's Sam

Belinda has sex with five people in one day. Were you worried that was too many?

When you're an author it's great to be lost in your own web of intrigue, plot development, and unique simile assessment. So you can see how simple it is to lose track of time and sexual activity. I hadn't actually realized I'd written that Belinda had had sex with five people in a day by the end of this chapter.

Belinda was getting a little bit hacked off with corporate life. I mean, she'd just had three chaps who were all worth a few million quid, why not enjoy a fling with a youngish chap who was obviously starting out in life? He could have his own hotel within three years . . . why wouldn't you???

Rocky x

♘ ACTIVITY

Groaning is repeatedly referred to in *Belinda Blinked 1* (as an indication of sexual fulfilment as opposed to representing displeasure at a bad joke).

With a partner (sexual or platonic), practice your nuanced groaning—try to express a variety of emotions only through guttural moaning and see if they can guess which you are performing.

Rocky's Turkey Sandwich Recipe

Ingredients:

White sliced bread

Salted butter

Turkey breast in thick slices

Salt

Method:

1. Butter the slices of bread thickly. Gently salt the thickly sliced turkey to taste.

2. Place the turkey thickly over the first slice of buttered bread.

3. Place the second buttered slice of bread over the top. Push down firmly.

4. Cut into three pieces and arrange delicately on a white plate. Serve.

(Q) KEY THEME: Alcohol

Alcohol is a recurring motif in *Belinda Blinked 1* and serves a number of literary functions—however, it is rarely used for its actual purpose of drinking. The two beverages that feature most heavily are gin and tonic and Chilean Chardonnay. Not coincidentally, these are two of Flintstone's favorite tipples. Gin and tonic is used flirtatiously by the women to tease their breasts through their wet blouses in Chapter 3. Furthermore, it is used for foreplay when the Duchess drinks tinned gin and tonic out of Belinda's vagina at the tombola. And, of course, it is used as a lubricant in this chapter when our heroine rubs wine over the Youngish Man's penis. Despite alcohol being used in these unusual scenarios, it is interesting to note that all the characters drink responsibly. This is most likely due to the fact that men find it harder to get and maintain an erection after prolonged heavy drinking.

(📖) Reading group discussion points

- Discuss your favorite late-night snacks.

- Does Belinda receive good customer service at the Horse and Jockey?

- As a group, decide what constitutes "the high life."

- What's the latest you've ever gone to bed?

- Share any late-night hotel anecdotes with the group.

- Would you feel shortchanged by a tit wank with a push-up bra?

Didn't Margaret Thatcher survive on only
four hours of sleep a night? Belinda for PM?

A dress is always in one piece. Otherwise it would be a skirt and top.

Oh, unless it's a one-piece because the bra and panties are attached
to the dress like a cheap shirt and T-shirt combo from Primark ...

Like a caged animal—return her to the wild.

Talking Point

Morality is a fluctuating concept throughout Flintstone's prose. Belinda is
undoubtedly a thief, yet here she redeems herself by returning the stolen
garments to the Duchess.

What does the inclusion of the word "reluctantly" tell us about Belinda's ethics?

CHAPTER 13;

The Duchess comes clean;

She must be knackered.

It was six thirty in the morning when Belinda awoke from her deep sleep. The receptionist had left at two thirty giving her a much needed <u>four hours sleep.</u> There was much to do and certainly no time for breakfast, even if it were being served by the very sexually fulfilled night receptionist called Sam. *FINALLY he gets a name. Just as she fucks off.*

This time Belinda dressed in one of her simple <u>one piece, black, work dresses</u> with matching lace bra and panties. Her plan was very simple. She would get back to the motel, release the Duchesses ankles from the yellow handcuffs, take her back to the chairman's house where she could collect her company car and get into work for nine. The Duchess could then collect her trailer from the motel and continue her sex life as she wanted... but without her involvement. Belinda would also reluctantly return the horse riding outfit which had served her extremely well all Sunday evening.

Surely she deserves a day in lieu for all this?

She was all over her a few chapters ago. Fickle Belinda.

179

She's hard as nails. He's been
inside you; at least say goodbye. _____

Thank God I'd heard horse
box theft was on the rise. _____

It's like a shit fairy tale. Belinda
is now Prince Charming. _____

No, that's not how it works. Plus
she has to be at work by nine. _____

Bull. Shit. She could have taken Belinda to
the motel and made her a nice cup of tea.
The riding crop was not necessary. _____

s. Because it's 6:30 in the morning, Belinda.

He'll always be the Youngish Man to me.

The traffic was nonexistent as she left the Horse and Jockey. Sam had obviously gone to kitchen duty so no time was lost in saying farewell. The company was picking up the tab on the overnight room and meals, so she got off to a good start. She quickly motored through the beautiful Oxfordshire countryside to the Motel where she had left the Duchess attached to her bed. The horsebox was still in the parking spot where she had left it and the motel room looked quiet.

But not that vat of wine she guzzled, surely?

Belinda jumped out of the big vehicle and entered the room. In the bedroom she found the Duchess where she had left her, albeit her make up now smeared to hell.

Handcuffs will do that.

Is she the "maniac with the taste for the dramatic"?

Belinda switched off the bedside light and gently shook the Duchess awake.

Like a rag doll?

'You've come back to release me.' was the first words she murmured.

'Yes.' said Belinda equally as softly, 'But you must understand that as I was your sex servant, so now you are mine.'

A bit late to recap the rules of the tombola.

The Duchess started to sob softly and replied,

Someone give the poor woman a hug and a hankie.

'I always knew it would come to this, I have to tell you, I was a very reluctant player in this erotic game, they left me no choice in the end, and now here I am… a sex servant to you, Miss Belinda.'

Who are "they"?? Could there be a plot after all?

181

Well, she was just about to tell you. _____

*In what world are the monikers "My lady"
and "Miss Belinda" equal?* _____

Cultural Context

Here the theme of feminism shines through. *Belinda Blinked 1* is the only known erotic novella that passes the Bechdel test.

The Bechdel test is a feminist benchmark developed by Alison Bechdel in 1985 for cinema. It states that there must be a scene in which two or more named female characters have a conversation about anything besides men.

*Does he mean "over the hill" or is she
just a really flamboyant lover?* _____

Run. For. The. Hills.
Keep on the handcuffs and get the hell out of there.

—Drink!

Belinda blinked, was this whole episode a game organized by someone else, was there a master planner behind all of the tombola activities and the ramifications they were producing. It certainly couldn't be coincidence that she, Bella and Giselle were the ones to be made servants. Perhaps the Duchess knew more than she was telling, she needed to proceed softly, she needed the Duchess on her side.

Obviously. She's a few turkeys short of a sandwich, our Belinda.

'If you can call me Miss Belinda then I can happily call you 'My Lady'. Is this a good start to an equal relationship between us?'

'I think so, yes I know so... oh how I do want to be a sexual servant to you Miss Belinda! I just want you to fuck me hard with my beautiful black leather dildo and respect me for what I am... a happy sex servant to you!'

This is a beautiful greeting card. Not.

'Well that's fine I suppose, from your perspective, but what do I get out of the relationship.' replied Belinda.

Sex.

The Duchess thought for a moment.

'I know that sexually I'm a bit over the top, age wise that is, but I do assure you I am a fanatical lover, and in my role as your sex servant I will do your every bidding. I am open to all new sex erotica and I promise to never disobey you in the sexual act. I will drink your orgasms, and eat your vagina all day long until you order me to stop.'

I'll never eat again.

I order you to stop.

You met her last night. And have barely spoken.

> **Talking Point**
>
> The theme of class becomes more pronounced as the novel progresses. In Chapter 1 Belinda is described as an "upmarket woman." By Chapter 7 she is knee-deep in mud and tied to a trellis. Here Belinda appears to have reached the pinnacle of her perceived sophistication.

Is that what happens when you're suddenly freed? Nelson Mandela's must have been smuggling peanuts.

> **Cultural Context**
>
> The *Titanic* was a luxury liner that infamously sank on its maiden voyage in 1912 after hitting an iceberg.
>
> In 1998 two of its wrought-iron rivets were recovered for scientific research. It was discovered that they were riddled with atypically high levels of slag, making them brittle and prone to fracture.

I'm imagining Belinda slamming into her nipples with force.

Belinda quickly interrupted and said,

'I get your intentions, and they are truly what I need of you if you wish to become my sex servant. But surely a person as well connected to the lineage of Britain, I mean you being a Duchess with all what that means, could surely open doors I couldn't dream of ever even encountering.'

Why has she turned into Nancy from Oliver!?

'Miss Belinda, I adore you so much, yes, I will be able to introduce you into the highest sexual circles in the land.'

Belinda bent over and pulled the plastic handcuffs off the Duchesses ankles. The Duchess stood up and stretched her cramped body. Her nipples hardened with her feeling of freedom and they were now as large as the three inch rivets which had held the hull of the fateful Titanic together. Belinda was drawn to them like a magnet, she needed to touch them, caress them and finally suck them. The Duchess stood still as Belinda fulfilled her desires. —*Tighten them with a spanner.*

Nothing says sexy like a cramp.

7.5cm-long nipples?!

After two minutes of caressing and sucking, the Duchess carefully removed Belinda's one piece black work dress. She then slowly removed her black lace bra and after a few moments her panties. Belinda stepped out of her high heels and guided the Duchess back to the bed.

Get a move on—you need to get to work.

Will it never end? Please let it end.

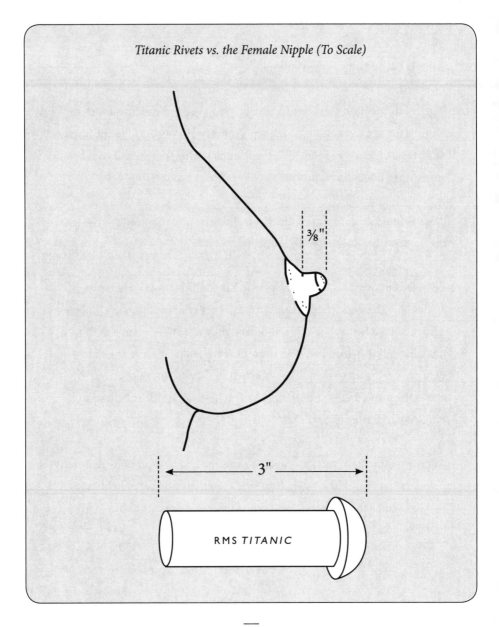

Titanic Rivets vs. the Female Nipple (To Scale)

¾"

3"

RMS *TITANIC*

CHARACTER PROFILE: Sir James Godwin

A character who is rarely mentioned, but who serves as the mysterious link between Belinda and her "sexual mistress" the Duchess, is Sir James Godwin. The chairman and chief executive of Steele's Pots and Pans, Sir James is a formidable character. He has high-society connections and as a Knight of the Realm has been known to move in royal circles.

His philanthropic work is substantial and varied, though the cause closest to his heart is that of the Asses and Donkeys Trust, of which is he is sole patron. He generously hosts the annual fund-raiser and tombola at his Oxfordshire country house, which boasts a medium-sized maze and a Roman style amphitheater. He also puts on a large BBQ. With chairs.

• **Physical Attribute:** Silver haired and suave

• **Dominant Character Trait:** Well-bred

• **Unusual Skill:** Donkey whisperer

• **Fun Fact:** His maze brings all the boys to the yard

🔓 KEY THEME: Naming Convention in Literature

Rocky Flintstone has a decidedly laissez-faire attitude to naming his characters; it took Belinda to be stripped naked for Tony to introduce himself in Chapter 1, for example. Indeed, throughout the novel the seductive victor of the tombola is known only as the Duchess. This ambiguity is typical of idiosyncratic novels and as such Flintstone is in good writerly company.

Fight Club by Chuck Palahniuk plays on the identity of protagonist Tyler Durden, ultimately rendering him nameless. Similarly, in Daphne du Maurier's masterpiece *Rebecca* the narrator remains as ghostly and illusive as the titular character haunting the Manderley estate. It appeared we were destined for another such character in the form of the Youngish Man until this chapter, when he is revealed to be called by the run-of-the-mill name Sam.

✏️ AUTHOR'S NOTE

The Duchess alludes to a conspiracy in this chapter, hinting at a bigger story to unfold. Where do you see Belinda's adventures taking her next?

You have to remember that the Duchess is related to the highest bloodline in the land, and because she holds this sense of duty it is natural that she will never be able to release her deepest secrets. As a commoner Belinda has no option but to pursue her line of questioning in the bedroom.

The future books are an ongoing diary of Belinda's daily job where she meets both international and UK-based characters in her mission to make Steele's the top pots-and-pans manufacturer in the world. Tony is very much on board with this strategy, but Sir James Godwin will require winning over as he is the one who takes the ultimate monetary risk. This source of tension continues to run through the company and causes unnecessary strife in Belinda's life . . .

Rocky x

ACTIVITY

Go round the group and reveal a secret about yourself. In the style of the Duchess, stop short of actually divulging any of the details.

Reading group discussion points

- Do you see any similarity between the doomed lovers Rose and Jack in *Titanic* and the Duchess and Belinda in *Belinda Blinked 1*?

- How far would you go to secure an invite to a high-society luncheon?

- Has there been an instance where you left a lover without saying goodbye?

Still wrong. If it's got a red squiggly line under it, don't press print.

Are they like the T&Cs no one EVER reads when you update iTunes?

CHAPTER 14

Monday Morning 7.45am

The last chapter and he's still making typos.

'My Lady, I feel I need to fulfill your strongest desires.'

'Yes, Miss Belinda, please do what you need to me, and then if you so desire please fuck me with the black leather dildo, hard, up my vagina and don't stop… if it pleases you, Miss Belinda.'

As opposed to what? Sideways?

'My Lady, it does please me and I shall fulfill your needs, but then you need to drive me back to my car so I can get to work and end this very strange weekend.'

Understatement of the millennium.

'Yes, I accept your terms, please buckle on the dildo and fuck me slowly… Miss Belinda.'

Sounds like she's on the waltzers.
Give that dildo a safety check.

Belinda walked over to the closet and took out the dildo. She carefully strapped it on making sure it was tight around her ass. The leather straps

I can't believe I'm learning how to attach a strap-on from my father.

They're the length of a credit card. ——————————

Love that Dad has given it a capital D.
Is it now a character? ——————

Who knew this would be an occupational hazard
in the pots-and-pans sector? ——————————

Is she fucking her or fracking her? ——————————

This reads as if Belinda's ——————————
munching on her own.

Not. A. Sensual. Word. ——————————

This is sex, not keyhole surgery. ——————

Is that the equivalent of straightening her thong? ——

No. It. Didn't. You're going left and right,
you're turning corners. Suddenly she's just one
big pinball machine.

Is she bulging out of it? It's all those turkey sandwiches.

and chrome buckles took the strain and the dildo was ready for action. The Duchess smiled and opened her legs wide as she lay back on the bed and let Belinda enter her slowly. Belinda lowered her head, her long black hair fell over the Duchesses breasts, she found the still extended nipples and started to chew them gently as she increased the friction on the Duchess's clitoris.

— Like a rat?

Good for a bit of purchase.

A low moan came from the bed, which increased in intensity as the two females maintained their rhythm; the Dildo was strapped on so tightly that Belinda felt its surging movement hit her pubic area each time she penetrated further into the Duchess. Meanwhile the Duchess had found Belinda's tits and was massaging her nipples as strongly as Belinda was chewing her own. The Duchess suddenly climaxed, her orgasm was even more infectious on Belinda, and she pushed the dildo harder into her cervix. Eventually Belinda came out as gently as she could, realigned the dildo and went in again. The Duchess steadied herself and let out a long sigh as the dildo hit her ovaries. Belinda pushed it further and further into her vagina, she leant forward and sucked the Duchess's tits and again started to ride her, hard.

Why are they having so much trouble locating things? They're not a Picasso painting.

Look behind you. You've gone so far the vagina is merely a dot.

Lest we forget, someone, somewhere, calls her granny.

'Please don't stop Miss Belinda, this is so good! The Duchess cried out in ecstasy.

'Yes My Lady... even I'm enjoying it, and soon it's going to be even better!'

Body in the bedroom. Mind in the office. ———

Well, they're paper thin so she's
really just scrunching them. ———

We're all being
punished. ———

Buyer's remorse there, ———
Belinda.

Oh God, what's in
there? Will Mr. Tumnus
be joining them? ———

Like an old shire horse after a long day toiling the fields.

Belinda had no idea how what she was doing was going to improve, but she was up for it for at least another ten minutes. The Duchess lasted only two minutes when she orgasmed and Belinda felt it was time to change tack. By now she herself was feeling extremely horny and standing up she unbuckled the dildo and threw it onto the floor.

What is this?

I'd rather have a Calippo.

'OK My Lady, it's your turn to please me… suck me all over!'

Maybe just wait for instruction.

Belinda lay down on the bed as the Duchess got onto her knees. Needing no further instruction the Duchess started to lick Belinda's breasts, her tongue snaked down to her pubic hair and followed the trail to her vagina. Meanwhile Belinda grabbed her servant's ample tits and started to rub them hard. The Duchess groaned, Belinda groaned as her clit started to be punished by the Duchess's tongue. A few minutes later, Belinda orgasmed, not once but twice, her mind went into turmoil, the deep sensations were too much for her. She struggled to regain consciousness and all she could murmur was,

Why does she have a hairy chest?

We all groaned.

How would her eulogy read if this was how she popped her clogs?

'Thank you My Lady, thank you My Lady.'

'Thank you Miss Belinda.' Was the only reply she received as the Duchess got up and went to the closet. 'It's time we finished this crazy weekend so let's get back to our real lives before we're missed!'

Oh thank God, this is all going to be a bad dream. And we're all going to wake up.

195

They'll share a dildo but they won't share a loofah. ———

Sounds like she can't
wait to escape. ———

'I agree, but what are you looking for?' replied Belinda.

Awkward.

'My riding gear… I know I had it with me, but don't worry, I've got my white linen suit right here… I'll wear that instead, the midday meeting at the Jockey Club doesn't require any formal wear… unless it's a dinner of course! She laughed and Belinda joined in, totally unaware of the etiquette of horse riding circles.

Totally blagging it. Belinda does not get the joke. And neither do I.

Belinda and the Duchess showered separately then dressed and prepared themselves for the day. While Belinda hooked up the horse box to the 4x4 the Duchess packed the leather dildo safely into its special zinc coated case, much like a professional photographer's camera. With the motel room cleared, the Duchess locked the door, left the keys at reception and started the engine of the big vehicle. In fairness she only scuffed one corner on the journey back to the country house where Belinda's Merc was parked.

It's not kryptonite.

She'll lose her no claims for that.

Belinda jumped out of the front passenger seat and said farewell to the Duchess. They had swopped email addresses and planned a reunion at a hotel on the Isle of Whyte in three weeks' time. It was a gala ball and the Duchess had promised to introduce her 'Sexual Mistress' to some new acquaintances. Belinda took out her car keys and opened the Merc. It started first time, she waved goodbye to the Duchess, who promptly accelerated off in a cloud of gravel and dust.

It's brand new, you'd hope so.

Bye then, Mad Max.

How very fitting for the last word to be "fucked." ——————

Belinda lost no time in following her and was in the office for a very respectable 9.30am. As she sat down at her desk, Belinda could only wonder what the next two weeks would hold for her, if they were anything like the last 24 hours, she would be truly <u>fucked</u>!

BELINDA'S CHARACTER ARC

When we meet Belinda, she is embarking on a new chapter in her life, in an area of business she hasn't experienced before. But, in her inimitable style, she secures the job of her dreams.

Initially trepidatious about the challenge facing her, she quickly grows in confidence, and over the course of a few days almost everyone at the office has seen her nipples, if not had sex with her.

At Steele's her skill set is truly tested; she is quite literally dragged through a hedge (maze) backwards, sold as a sex slave to a member of the British upper classes, and is carted around in a horse box. But within weeks she has secured big-ticket sales with some major European operators—totalling 5,000 units—and has made some great alliances and contacts for further negotiations.

Personally she has made great bonds too: her relationship with Peter has a promising future (bar his pesky wife) and she has a great e-penpal in the Duchess.

What's next, we don't know, and until he puts pen to paper, perhaps neither does Flintstone.

⊕ KEY THEME: The British Aristocracy

Though the role of the British aristocracy has been drastically diminished in the modern era, well-bred members of the establishment still hold great influence and power within society. Unelected peers occupy the Upper Chamber of Parliament, and the monarch biannually bestows honors on to the most worthy citizens of the land.

Public schools educate the elite of British society, with students often boarding at extortionate termly cost. The alumni of such institutions include past kings and prime ministers, and great folklore surrounds them to this day. One particular myth is that of the "soggy biscuit" game. Participants engage in group masturbation around a biscuit, ejaculating on to it en masse. The final pupil to do so must eat the creamed cookie as punishment.

✎ AUTHOR'S NOTE

What was your writing process while penning *Belinda Blinked 1*?

Without giving away any spoiler alerts I write to a very defined plot line. I call it a timeline and it's basically the skeleton upon which I put on . . . or take off . . . the clothing of the characters and what they get up to each day. It actually means it's super easy to write the books. My timelines come to me when I'm awake in bed around 3:00 a.m. in the morning. *Bammm*—an idea just hits me and then I can get back to sleep.

Rocky x

 **ACTIVITY**

Trade email addresses with the next stranger you encounter and become penpals. You must exchange correspondence at least three times a year for the next five.

Reading group discussion points

- How has Belinda changed your life?

- Looking at *Belinda Blinked 1* in its literary context, which novels and authors would you compare it to?

- Discuss what you've learned about sex from Rocky Flintstone.

- What passage of *Belinda Blinked 1* can't you forget?

- What are your hopes for Belinda's future?

- Whatever happened to Bill?

When Rocky Flintstone first sold his e-book to the world he crafted a compelling blurb with which to seduce the online market. Below is what made *Belinda Blinked 1* truly stand out in the saturated sea of self-penned erotica.

Least sexy name EVER.

Great start, Dad; already a typo.

BLURB:

Belinda Blumenthal gets exciting, sollicited sex regularly, so regularly *Oh, that London.* in fact she makes big bonuses from it. Based in London UK, Belinda works for Steeles Pots and Pans as their world wide Sales Director. Sexually *This has to be the first erotic novel about kitchenware.* supported by Giselle and Bella her head office colleagues, Belinda always gets the order when it comes down to the bare facts. The client base is large so Belinda has the whole world to fuck and boy does she get stuck *Already dropped the F-bomb. Great.* into it. This is the first book in the Belinda Blinked series where she gets hired by Tony her Managing Director and then goes on to make some sales *Oh no. Series means at least three.* headway by bringing on board a large European customer, Peter Rouse, and makes initial inroads to the North American market through Jim Stirling. Read about the sexual conquests these men make and how the mysterious Duchess makes Belinda alive to the sexual fantasies of the hot riding set through supple black riding boots, jodhpurs and leather handled whips....

If this was on the back of the book I wouldn't have bought it. So boring.

ROCKY'S PROFILE:

Rocky likes to write in the sun and with a glass of wine in his hand. Nothing makes him feel more at home. Based between Brazil and Marbella Spain he gets to grips with his stories, bringing them to print for his loyal readers. *Belinda Blinked 1* is his first novel of the series and Rocky has just completed his second, *Belinda Blinked 2.*

Steele's Pots & Pans

COMPANY STRUCTURE

Steele's is an international conglomerate with a focus on the pots-and-pans corner of the retail market. The corporation's hierarchy is similar to many sales operations, however uniquely you are able to ascend from PA to MD in five years.

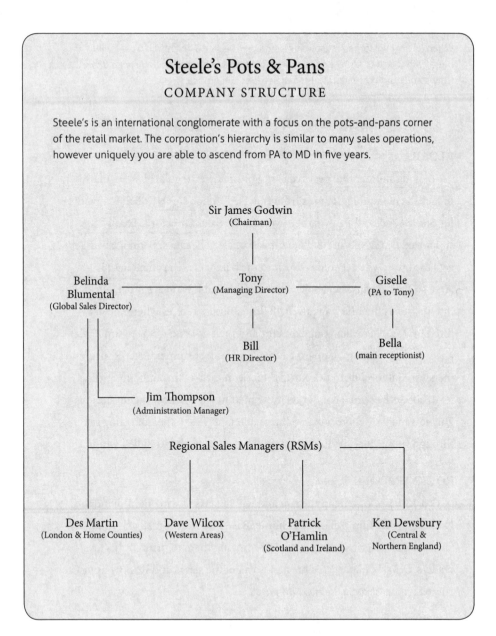

Sir James Godwin
(Chairman)

Belinda Blumental
(Global Sales Director)

Tony
(Managing Director)

Giselle
(PA to Tony)

Bill
(HR Director)

Bella
(main receptionist)

Jim Thompson
(Administration Manager)

Regional Sales Managers (RSMs)

Des Martin
(London & Home Counties)

Dave Wilcox
(Western Areas)

Patrick O'Hamlin
(Scotland and Ireland)

Ken Dewsbury
(Central & Northern England)

Belinda's Sex Tree

Within the world of *Belinda Blinked 1*, sexuality is fluid and sexual relations are prolific. Here's a handy reference to the carnal connections made throughout the course of the novel.

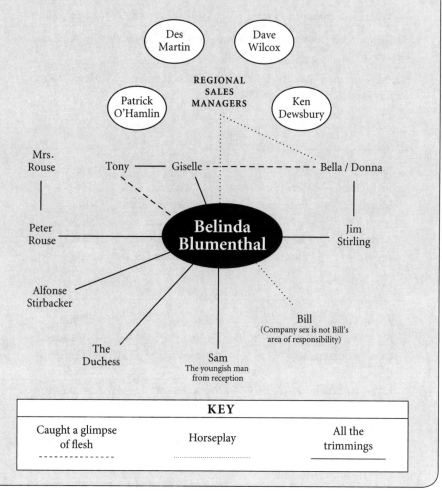

KEY		
Caught a glimpse of flesh	Horseplay	All the trimmings
- - - - - - - - - - -	··················	———————

My Dad Wrote a Porno
THE PORN PEN NAME GENERATOR

Rocky Flintstone's anonymity is maintained with the shrewd use of his pseudonym.

To find your perfect nom de porn, just like Rocky, use our simple Porn Pen Name Generator.

Here's the equation: Month of birth + first initial of the person you'd like to take in the Leather Room = your erotic alias.

FIRST NAME

January	–	Rambo	July	–	Maverick
February	–	Terminator	August	–	Blade
March	–	Robocop	September	–	Cobra
April	–	Apollo	October	–	Chuck
May	–	Jean Claude	November	–	Indiana
June	–	Flash	December	–	Dredd

SURNAME

A	–	Oil	J	–	Boop	S	–	Fudd
B	–	Rubble	K	–	De Vil	T	–	Haddock
C	–	Squarepants	L	–	the Explorer	U	–	Gadget
D	–	Jetson	M	–	Le Pew	V	–	Sneer
E	–	McDuck	N	–	Woodpecker	W	–	Gummi
F	–	Dinkley	O	–	Slaghoople	X	–	Brown
G	–	Dastardly	P	–	Leghorn	Y	–	Griffin
H	–	O'Hare	Q	–	Cartman	Z	–	Simpson
I	–	Pitstop	R	–	Gonzales			

My Dad Wrote a Porno

THE DRINKING GAME

"Fun for all the family" . . . is something that has never been said about *Belinda Blinked 1*. The same is true of this game. Gather your least bashful friends and enjoy a night as thrilling as a lock-in at the Pentra.

The only drinks approved by Belinda are Chilean Chardonnay and gin and tonic, but feel free to introduce beverages of your choosing—just ensure that there are enough impeccable glasses for all.

Drinks can be consumed the traditional way (via the mouth) or à la Belinda and the Duchess (via a vagina).

Allocate each player a key *Belinda Blinked 1* theme from the list, then when it arises, bottoms up! All four of them!

For more players, allocate themes in pairs.

THEMES

1. **Nipples** (including rivets or general breast references)

2. **Items of clothing being removed** (double-drink if it's done gently, swiftly, or deftly)

3. **Business jargon** (including contractual details and mundane corporate chat)

4. **Genitalia, female** (including vaginal lids, labial pinkness, and cervix)

5. **Genitalia, male** (double-drink if you can find Jim Stirling's)

6. **Thongs**

7. **Kissing** (anywhere)

8. **Stroking or sexual touching**

9. **New characters**

10. **When Belinda speaks** (for the lightweight of the group)

   Everyone drinks when Belinda blinks!

My Dad Wrote a Porno
THE QUIZ

Belinda didn't get asked a single question in the interview for the job of her dreams, so this test is far more rigorous than her final interview at Steele's. See how well you know the cast of characters, plot points, and literary motifs of *Belinda Blinked 1* with this handy revision quiz. When you're done, rate yourself:

1-10 correct = Not even quite as smart as Bella/Donna

11-20 correct = You're as bad as the Duchess is at driving

21-30 correct = A shrewd entrepreneur, you're an Alfonse in the making

31-40 correct = A BTEC in Business for you, like the Youngish Man is currently studying for

Over 40 correct = Genius. Belinda would shag you to congratulate you

1. How many times is the word "tit" or "tits" used in the text?

2. What are the first two words of *Belinda Blinked 1*?

3. What color was Belinda's brassiere in the job interview?

4. What material were the elegant coat hooks made of in the job interview?

5. What color was the leather seat Belinda was gently sweating on?

6. What job is Belinda interviewing for at Steele's Pots and Pans?

7. What is the job offer on the table?

8. Where does the runnel of vaginal liquid go in the job interview?

9. What is the name of the Human Resources Director who suddenly appears in the job interview?

10. What two ages does Flintstone give to Giselle in the book?

11. What nationality is Giselle?

12. What is Bella's job title at Steele's Pots and Pans?

13. What does Tony tell Belinda to wear for the chairman's country house event?

14. How much time passes between Chapter 1 and 2 of the book?

15. In whose office can the Leather Room be found?

16. What is the only item of furniture in the Leather Room?

17. After their brief dalliance in Chapter 2, when did Bella and Belinda arrange to meet privately for more sex?

18. True or false? Belinda has a briefcase.

19. What make is Belinda's work car?

20. How long does it take Belinda to drive from the office to her central London apartment?

21. Which Regional Sales Manager is responsible for central and northern England?

A: Patrick O'Hamlin
B: Dave Wilcox
C: Des Martin
D: Ken Dewsbury

22. Why can't the Regional Sales Managers get a taxi from Heathrow?

23. What is the name of the pub the RSMs go to for lunch with Belinda?

24. When was the last time Belinda says she saw a pair of red plastic handcuffs?

25. What country is Alfonse Stirbacker from?

26. How many outlets is the Yankee Jim Stirling responsible for?

A: 320
B: 617
C: 1,257
D: 2,184

27. What does Jim Stirling do as soon as he has cum?

28. What state is Jim Stirling from?

29. Name four of Belinda's body parts that Peter draws symbols on (point for each).

30. What hairstyle does Peter craft Belinda's hair into with his semen?

31. Who is in Belinda's "glee team" (point for each)?

32. What is the Tombola's safeword? (For a bonus point, why is this safeword chosen?)

33. What was Belinda's number on her chair at the Tombola?

34. How much does Bella go for in the Tombola? (For a bonus point, who is the winning bidder?)

35. How does the Duchess demand to be addressed by Belinda?

36. How many times does Belinda make the Duchess orgasm with the leather dildo in the chalet?

37. What does Belinda think she looks like dressed in all the horse riding gear?

38. What time does dinner stop being served at the Horse and Jockey?

39. Which of the following items was NOT made of leather?
    A: The settee in the lobby of the Horse and Jockey
    B: The Duchess's dildo
    C: Jim Stirling's black thong
    D: The Duchess's riding boots

40. How many units of the Oxy Brillo range does Peter Rouse order?

41. How long does it take Peter Rouse to remove his clothes at the Horse and Jockey?

42. Belinda draws a figure of eight on Peter's stomach using what alcohol?

43. Complete this saying of Belinda's: "When you get what you want . . ."

44. What room service does the Youngish Man bring to Belinda's room?

45. What is the name of the Youngish Man?

46. What is the Duchess's dildo case coated with?

47. What time is Belinda aiming to be at work on Monday morning?

48. What time does Belinda actually arrive at work?

49. Which of these items was NOT black?
    A: Alfonse Stirbacker's thong
    B: Belinda's one-piece work dress
    C: The Duchess's cravat
    D: The Duchess's jodhpurs

50. How many times in the text does Belinda blink?

A: 7

B: 11

C: 14

D: 17